Kissing Atticus Primble

Stephanie Hoina

Whimsical Publications, LLC

Florida

Kissing Atticus Primble is a work of fiction. Names, characters, and incidents are the products of the author's imagination and are either fictitious or are used fictitiously. Any resemblance to actual events or persons, living or dead, is entirely coincidental.

To purchase the authorized electronic edition of *Kissing Atticus Primble*, visit
www.whimsicalpublications.com

Cover art by Traci Markou
Editing by Janet Durbin

ISBN-13: 978-1-940707-10-5

Published by
Whimsical Publications, LLC
Florida

"Who would you kiss...like that?" Abby had never been one to beat around the bush.

I blushed. At that very moment, I had been thinking about the way Bobby kissed Sara and wondered what it felt like to kiss him.

Seizing upon my discomfort, she badgered, "Come on, tell me! Who? Who?"

"No one," I lied, embarrassed by the physical betrayal of my thoughts.

Then, for a brief second, Atticus' face flashed before my eyes and my embarrassment faded to confusion.

"Fine, don't tell me," Abby admonished. "I know who it is anyway," she said confidently.

"Abby, there's nothing to tell." I defended my lack of reply. I shared almost everything with Abby. Not as much as I used to with Atticus, but close. If there was someone I wanted to kiss, I'd tell her. Maybe.

"Kathleen, everyone wants to kiss Bobby O'Hara," she said confidently, and we continued the rest of the way in silence.

That night, alone in my room, I considered Abby's question again. Did I want to kiss anyone the way Bobby kissed Sara? Did I want to kiss Bobby O'Hara? It was all a little scary if you ask me. This was exactly the kind of stuff that made me miss Atticus. Whenever something was bothering me, I could count on Atticus to make me feel better. But it had been a long time since we'd shared anything more than the most casual of exchanges. What would Atticus think about all this kissing stuff? As far as I knew, he hadn't kissed anyone yet. Did boys feel scared about it too?

Instinctively, I reached for my phone but changed my mind; he felt too far away. I had no idea when the last time I'd called him or even sent a text was. I needed my best friend back.

At graduation, he finally came around.

"No tears for you?" came his familiar voice off to my right. Atticus glanced around the gym, surveying the crying fest among the 8th grade girls. I followed his eyes and smiled at the scene, shrugging in response. Abby was nearly inconsolable, but she had always been overly emotional. I was pretty sure Abby, being Abby, simply loved the drama of it all.

She caught my eye and came over to Atticus and me.

"I can't believe it," she sniffled as she hugged me. "High school next year."

As she bent to hug Atticus, a fresh round of tears filled her eyes; she hugged him a little tighter with each sob. Atticus looked at me helplessly, and I could see him mentally counting the seconds until she released him.

Abby composed herself and made a beeline for Timmy Sheridan, her latest crush. She was launching herself into his arms just as Atticus' question reclaimed my attention.

"Are you going to Sara's party tonight?" he asked. The déjà vu of it all hit me; I nodded my reply. Sara's invitations were still pink and still sparkly, and her parties were still exclusive. I surmised correctly that Atticus and his friends hadn't been invited. He wasn't friends with Sara, and didn't care to be. But Atticus still saw the question in my eyes.

"A bunch of us are going to David's house later on. You know, a wild night of Dungeons and Dragons and Star Trek movies," he teased. But I knew better than that. Atticus' circle of friends was an interesting mix of kids, and they did more than play card games and watch movies. I was glad he had plans for the night as well.

We stood there silently while all around us people were hugging and crying and laughing and congratulating one another. Without thinking, I reached for his hand; he squeezed mine tightly in his grasp.

Maybe it was the prospect of a new beginning at a new school, a shared memory tugging at the corner of our brains. The fact we had grown apart those last couple of years didn't seem to matter now. A single tear rolled down my right cheek. For the moment, Atticus was back.

Acknowledgements

I started writing this acknowledgement before Kissing Atticus Primble was even finished. Before I knew whether it would ever find its way into an editor's heart, a bookstore's shelves, or a reader's hands.

I have always found acknowledgements to be a little publication of their own. For example, I noticed that Nicholas Sparks tells a story before you even start his novels—the story of all the people who helped him get where he is today. He is funny and self-deprecating and genuinely appreciative.

So, here's my story, because I have those people too, without whom this never would have happened.

First and foremost, a big thank you to Lee Harper, an incredible illustrator and friend. You got me started on Atticus. What else can I say?

To Facebook, for giving me a platform to share excerpts of this story with a few hundred friends, many of whom became as invested in the lives of Kathleen and Atticus as I was. They urged me to keep writing, to let them know what happens. I never would have finished without you and couldn't have asked for better cheerleaders...you know who you are.

To Mark McGrath, an author himself, who suggested I send my story to his publisher, because "I think she will like it." And she did. Thank you, Janet Durbin, for "liking it" and giving me this wonderful opportunity. (Oh, and for your patience and guidance during the editing phase!)

To my parents. Although my dad is no longer with us, his unconditional love and pride in even my minor accomplishments always helped me feel a little special. That "specialness" translated into a belief that I just might be able to do anything I really put my mind to. And my mom, whose adolescent poetry (which I found as a little girl tucked away in a drawer in our china cabinet) inspired me. She never had the opportunity to explore her literary dreams, but sacrificed much to allow me mine. Thank you both for letting me spread my wings even though sometimes I was afraid to fly.

To my husband, Ron, who has always been my champion. When, twenty-five years ago, I told you the only thing standing in the way of my writing was a computer, you bought me one, no questions asked (and they were ridiculously expensive twenty-five years ago!) Though it turned out the only thing really standing in the way of my writing was "me." Your confidence in my ability has never waned. You are my best friend and biggest supporter and I'm so happy we get to experience this moment together—one of many amazing moments we have been lucky enough to share over the course of 30 years. I know many more await us. "It had to be you" then—and it still is you now.

A very special thank you to my son, Zac. As a little boy, when someone asked him what his mom did for a living, he would simply say, "she writes books." He believed it—even though I had nothing finished or close to being published. Well, here it is Zac, my first book! Your belief in me helps me to believe in myself. I love you more.

And lastly, to Lady Luck. Because there are many talented, hardworking people out there, trying to make their dream happen. I am fortunate she decided to shine her light on me.

Prologue

Maybe following Atticus Primble into the boys' bathroom wasn't the best of ideas. School rules most definitely frowned upon it, and so apparently did Atticus. But when you're a 16-year-old girl in love for the first time, well, in REAL love for the first time, you don't pay much attention to the student handbook or the privacy concerns of the object of your affection. You only pay attention to the ache in your heart and the overwhelming need to logically explain at just that very minute why you had to see if you liked kissing Bobby O'Hara more than you liked kissing Atticus Primble.

Some things just can't wait!

Chapter One

The first day of kindergarten didn't frighten me. I was an academic veteran, having already survived two years of nursery school and one year of pre-school under the tutelage of the nuns at Saint Mary by the Shore.

From the look on his face, it appeared as if Atticus had never stepped foot into a classroom before. He promptly fell ill.

"Kathleen, please show our new student the way to the nurse's office," Sr. James requested, her stiff demeanor betrayed by the kindness and concern in her aquamarine eyes.

I headed down the hall with Atticus in tow.

"I feel like I'm going to throw up right now," said my pale-faced charge.

Luckily for Atticus, or was it for me, the boys' bathroom was only a few feet away.

"Quick, in there!" I pushed him through the door, stumbling in right behind him.

Atticus didn't move once we were inside, so neither did I. I looked around because he just kept doing nothing and I didn't know what else to do. Besides, I was curious. I had never been in the boys' bathroom before.

I remember thinking it was odd that they had two different kinds of sinks, and I wondered why they needed the second one. Maybe being as messy as they were, boys needed all the help they could get. Other than that, it looked pretty much like the girls' bathroom, except all the tiles were blue. I liked the blue tiles. I thought they were much nicer than the pink ones in the girls' bathroom.

To my mom's annoyance, I never really liked pink. I had two older brothers, and, according to my grandmother, my mother had been waiting a long time to dress a baby in pink. She got her wish until I turned three, then she had to settle for purple if she ever wanted to make it out of the house in a timely fashion. Grandma told me this story too, though I don't remember it. I think it broke my mom's heart a little.

Anyway, it only took me a few seconds to scope out the boys' room. I was already bored with it. And bored with Atticus.

"Well?" I asked. "Are you going to throw up or what?" That's what we were there for, after all, and I was tired of waiting.

Atticus looked at me with the oddest expression. As if he was expecting me to say something else.

Then he just smiled and said, "I like you. Will you be my friend?"

No one had ever asked me to be their friend before. It never occurred to me that anyone would ever need to ask that.

I was about to answer when the bathroom door swung open. A high-pitched voice sang out, "Oh *there* you are, Kathleen! What on heaven's earth are you doing in *here*?"

Though Atticus never actually got sick that day, the nuns were quite astonished to find me in the bathroom with him. They quickly shooed me out for reasons that escaped my ability to comprehend at the time. I just knew they weren't pleased about it.

I wasn't overly impressed with the boys' bathroom, but I liked Atticus. I decided to tell him at snack time I would be his friend.

Atticus and I didn't just become friends. We became the best of friends. Even as we got older and became more interested in endeavors better suited for our gender, we still sought each other out to share the details of our day, our thoughts, and our hearts.

My best girlfriends, who took it upon themselves to know better than I about everything, often questioned my loyalty to Atticus. It was hard for them to understand. There was so much he couldn't do, or so they said. Oh, did I fail to mention Atticus was in a wheelchair? I always seem to do that because that's not how I saw him. I never have. The first thing I remember noticing about Atticus was his eyes. He had the most piercing blue eyes I had ever seen, more blue on that day in kindergarten because his face was so pale, but they always stood out, even on days when his cheeks were a ruddy red from the cold or a golden tan from the sun. The secret to Atticus' charm for me had always been hidden in those eyes.

The fact that his legs did not work quite right never seemed to matter much to me. We still raced to the bus stop after school and laughed at my mom's old comic books. We still struggled over fractions in math, got bored to tears over history and looked forward to Christmas and birthdays and summer vacation. Atticus could swim as long as I helped him into the pool and dance as long as I gave him a fairly wide berth. Maybe he couldn't ice skate, but neither could Johnny Harper and his legs worked fine. Maybe he couldn't play basketball on our school team, but he still managed to get the ball in the hoop from the foul line more often during gym than anyone not on the basketball team. So you see, I didn't really notice the wheelchair.

To me, he was simply my friend Atticus, and always would be.

Being friends with Atticus wasn't always easy, though. Especially as we got older and further away from the protection offered by well-meaning parents who did their best to ensure that Atticus was never left out. There comes a point in time when a child recognizes they were being included because someone's mom made the guest list and not because the pleasure of their company had specifically been requested by the party girl or boy.

For Atticus, this realization came in the 6th grade.

Sara Midland, the most popular girl in my class, had invited me, Kathleen Marie Kearney, to my first ever boy-girl party. I suspected it had something to do with my mom being on the PTA with hers, as Sara hadn't spoken more than ten words to me all year. But that didn't matter. I was staring at the, ewwww, pink glitter-embossed invitation with *my* name neatly printed across the top. Saturday at 7 pm. A night party! Life couldn't get any better.

So, as we have done every day for the last seven years when the dismissal bell rang, Atticus and I made our way to the bus stop, recounting our day. I couldn't wait to talk to him about the party. I knew it was a first for him, too, and he was bound to be as excited, even though boys didn't show it as much.

I was literally bouncing down the sidewalk. Atticus' blue eyes seemed to dance with curiosity. He tilted his head and eyed me up and down. "What's up with you?"

I laughed at his question because of course he already suspected why I was so happy.

"The party, silly," I answered, leaving out the requisite, "Duh."

Those blue eyes stared at me blankly. My heart stopped, but just for a second.

"Oh please, Atticus, Sara's party. Don't tease me for being so excited. I know you're looking forward to it, too!"

Still a blank look from Atticus. And then I knew. Something had changed for us. Something beyond our control.

Atticus knew, too.

Perhaps he was more prepared for it, having actually lived his life versus merely being a part of it. He never talked about the differences he experienced. With me, there had never been any. He told me once the reason he asked me to be his friend that day in the bathroom was because I didn't ask about the wheelchair. Other kids always did. As if that's all they saw. To him, I was okay because I only saw a kid who was supposed to be throwing up.

In time, he did tell me about what happened, how when he was two, a drunk driver slammed into his mother's car and changed his life forever. Although he couldn't recall much before that day, he had vague memories of running in the grass or trying to ride a bright red tricycle. He wasn't sure if they were real or simply fabricated from pictures his mom had shown him, but those images could summon the feel of his legs working and somehow that was enough for him. But his accident wasn't where we started, and we never talked about it again.

I didn't know what to say about the party. So Atticus spoke first.

"It's okay, Katie." Atticus was the only person who ever called me that, but only when I was sad. "I'm not friends with Sara anyway."

I decided not to point out that neither was I. Atticus knew that already.

"I won't go." It killed me to say it. We both knew how much I really wanted to go. But it killed me a little more to think Atticus wasn't included. For the first time since we'd been friends, I wondered what else he'd been left out of without my knowing it. How much he had hidden from me.

Atticus shook his head. "Of course you'll go. Don't be silly. I don't want to go anyway. I can't dance to the music Sara likes."

His good humor warmed my heart. I would never have another friend like Atticus. And I would never truly deserve him. My going to the party changed things for us, but we were too young to realize the significance.

Sara's party was actually a lot of fun. I went with my friend Abby. We had known each other since the first grade. Not counting Atticus, she was my closest friend.

When we got there, the boys were standing on one side, the girls on the other. It was obvious that arrangement wouldn't last for long as evidenced by the furtive glances and stifled giggles coming from either side. Mrs. Midland turned on the music and Abby and I started to dance.

Sara pulled Bobby O'Hara out of the group. Although he protested loudly, I could tell he was glad she did. All the boys liked Sara. I even think Atticus had a crush on her, though he'd never admit it to me.

I didn't really like Sara all that much, but I was secretly glad to have been invited because all of the popular kids were there. I wondered if my being there made me popular by association. Abby said it did. I chose not to argue the point. I wanted to be popular. What 6th grade girl didn't?

Bobby and Sara were dancing right next to Abby and me, the only boy-girl couple in the room. I noticed Bobby looking at me every now and then, and worried that my dancing wasn't quite "popular" girl caliber. I wanted to sit down and hide my embarrassment, but Abby was twirling away, lost in the music and I knew she'd be mad if I left her.

When the song ended, I dragged Abby to one of the couches and we sat down. Bobby followed and sat down next to me. Sara stayed on the dance floor, but I could feel her eyes focused on us like a laser beam.

"You're a good dancer," Bobby said, his smile making me uncomfortable in a way I couldn't explain.

"Thanks. That's one of my favorite songs," I said, even though I had never heard it before.

I sat there not knowing what to say or do next. My heart was racing. Bobby was just sitting there, smiling. I was just sitting there, feeling sick. Sara saved me.

"Come on, Bobby. I like this song," she said, grabbing his hand and pulling him back toward the area that had been cleared for dancing.

Bobby looked at me and shrugged. Abby looked at me and shook her head.

"I can't believe you let her do that!" she admonished.

"Let her do what?" I asked.

"He likes you," she said shaking her head slowly from side to side. "Why didn't *you* dance with him?"

Liked me? No one had ever liked me before. Well, maybe Jason Shepherd in the 3rd grade, but Jason liked every girl in the 3rd grade! I was more than certain that Bobby O'Hara did not like me. Everyone knew he had liked Sara forever.

Sara and I were nothing alike. She was dark and mysterious with beautiful green eyes and jet-black hair. I was fair, pasty really, and blue-eyed with mousy blonde hair. I blended in with the crowd. She stood out like a shiny beacon on a dark night. She was bubbly and vivacious. I was quiet and reserved. She was smart and conscientious about her grades, I was glad to get the occasional "A", never working to the potential my teachers always saw in me. Oh, and she was a cheerleader. Didn't that say it all? So, as you can see, Bobby couldn't possibly like me.

But he did keep looking in my direction.

The party was over by eleven. Abby was sleeping over my house and we spent the better part of an hour going over every inch of the night in considerable detail. Abby insisted on bringing up the Bobby O'Hara incident, but I did my best to steer the conversation in a different direction. She would not be swayed.

"Did you see the way he was looking at you?" She giggled, a dreamy look in her eyes.

I had seen it. It made me self-conscious. I wasn't used to boys paying much attention to me, except Atticus.

But it was exciting. The thought that Bobby O'Hara, star player on our junior high basketball team, even though he was only a sixth grader, and arguably one of the cutest boys in school, might think I was pretty.

Abby and I fell asleep after a spirited exchange on the merits of being liked by Bobby O'Hara.

After Sara's party, I learned that she and Bobby were officially going steady. Bobby O'Hara barely spoke to me again.

I didn't even notice because after that night, Atticus seemed to withdraw a little into a world where I wasn't invited, and I cared more about being in Atticus' world than Bobby O'Hara's.

We started to move in different circles. For a time, we still found each other at the end of every day, perhaps to reassure ourselves that even though so much was changing in our lives and our bodies, there was a place we could go to be who we always were.

Atticus was invited to parties, but not usually the same ones as me. I guess you could say I was in the popular group and Atticus wasn't. At first I was angry because I thought he was being excluded due to his difference. Turns out, he *was* being excluded because he was different, but not because of his wheelchair. It was his attitude.

He wasn't nice to my friends. He thought they were silly and stupid and cared about things that weren't important. He thought he was better than them. Sometimes, when it was just the two of us, he was the same old Atticus. But around my friends, he could really be a jerk. I tried to talk to him about it, but he said I would never understand, which hurt my feelings. A lot. Eventually I stopped trying so hard.

It was the first time I could remember feeling so separated from Atticus, and I sometimes found it difficult to navigate life without him solidly by my side. He was the person I told everything to. *Everything*. There were no boundaries, no taboo subjects, nothing I felt uncomfortable sharing with him. When I first got my period, even though Abby had preceded me in that rite of passage, it was Atticus I told first. Granted, he wasn't particularly interested in the details I ultimately shared with Abby, but telling him felt as natural as sharing jokes about our favorite TV shows.

I often wondered if he missed our connection as much as I did. Atticus seemed happy enough hanging out with a new group of friends. I knew all of them, but they seemed to take his lead when it came to mixing with my new social circle. That's when I came to realize Atticus and I had drifted along together for a long time, to the exclusion of everyone else. Maybe that hadn't always been for the best. Truth be told, I was having fun with my ever-widening circle of friends. There was always something going on somewhere, either at school, in town, or at someone's house, and I liked being a part of it—well, a part of most of it.

Apparently, 8th grade was the year of the great "coupling." I say this because by then Sara and Bobby had been an item for a while, and little by little more of my classmates began to pair off into not so subtle relationships. Abby was fascinated by it, but I was secretly terrified. Kissing games like spin the bottle and seven minutes in heaven started making frequent appearances at random get-togethers, which I did my best to avoid playing whenever possible. There was absolutely no one I wanted to kiss like *that*. Thankfully, Abby was in no rush either, though she professed to be in love with a different boy every week, and the whole kissing thing was never far from her thoughts, even if her lips hadn't experienced it yet.

"So, how far past kissing do you think they've gone?" she asked one day out of the blue as we were having lunch in the cafeteria.

"How far has who gone?" I asked, though the trickle of laughter from the rest of the table made it clear I was the only one in the dark about who Abby meant.

Abby rolled her eyes playfully and let me in on the secret.

"Bobby and Sara."

I looked around the table feeling incredibly naive.

"You think they've done more than kissed?" I asked innocently. I mean after all they were only fourteen.

My question was greeted with more laughter from my lunch mates.

"I don't know," said Abby. "They've been going out for almost two years. Have you ever seen the way they kiss?"

Yes, I had seen the way they kissed. *Because they kissed all over the place*. I tried to look away but it simply wasn't possible. My curiosity always got the best of me. As a result, I became an expert at secret sidelong glances. Yes, I had most certainly seen the way they kissed.

"You think they've...done...*it?*" I let the question hang in the air.

Some of the other girls at the table nodded but Abby just shrugged and said, "Who knows." And just like that she was on to a new topic of conversation.

I was still thinking about it all as we walked out of the school towards the pizzeria.

Abby was rambling on about her new crush, Timmy Sheridan. When she noticed I wasn't paying attention, she surprised me with another question.

"Who would you kiss...like that?" Abby had never been one to beat around the bush.

I blushed. At that very moment, I had been thinking about the way Bobby kissed Sara and wondered what it felt like to kiss him.

Seizing upon my discomfort, she badgered, "Come on, tell me! Who? Who?"

"No one," I lied, embarrassed by the physical betrayal of my thoughts.

Then, for a brief second, Atticus' face flashed before my eyes and my embarrassment faded to confusion.

"Fine, don't tell me," Abby admonished. "I know who it is anyway," she said confidently.

"Abby, there's nothing to tell." I defended my lack of reply. I shared almost everything with Abby. Not as much as I used to with Atticus, but close. If there was someone I wanted to kiss, I'd tell her. Maybe.

"Kathleen, everyone wants to kiss Bobby O'Hara," she

said confidently, and we continued the rest of the way in silence.

That night, alone in my room, I considered Abby's question again. Did I want to kiss anyone the way Bobby kissed Sara? Did I want to kiss Bobby O'Hara? It was all a little scary if you ask me. This was exactly the kind of stuff that made me miss Atticus. Whenever something was bothering me, I could count on Atticus to make me feel better. But it had been a long time since we'd shared anything more than the most casual of exchanges. What would Atticus think about all this kissing stuff? As far as I knew, he hadn't kissed anyone yet. Did boys feel scared about it too?

Instinctively, I reached for my phone but changed my mind; he felt too far away. I had no idea when the last time I'd called him or even sent a text was. I needed my best friend back.

At graduation, he finally came around.

"No tears for you?" came his familiar voice off to my right. Atticus glanced around the gym, surveying the crying fest among the 8th grade girls. I followed his eyes and smiled at the scene, shrugging in response. Abby was nearly inconsolable, but she had always been overly emotional. I was pretty sure Abby, being Abby, simply loved the drama of it all.

She caught my eye and came over to Atticus and me.

"I can't believe it," she sniffled as she hugged me. "High school next year."

As she bent to hug Atticus, a fresh round of tears filled her eyes; she hugged him a little tighter with each sob. Atticus looked at me helplessly, and I could see him mentally counting the seconds until she released him.

Abby composed herself and made a beeline for Timmy Sheridan, her latest crush. She was launching herself into his arms just as Atticus' question reclaimed my attention.

"Are you going to Sara's party tonight?" he asked. The déjà vu of it all hit me; I nodded my reply. Sara's invitations were still pink and still sparkly, and her parties were still exclusive. I surmised correctly that Atticus and his friends hadn't been invited. He wasn't friends with Sara, and didn't care to be. But Atticus still saw the question in my eyes.

"A bunch of us are going to David's house later on. You know, a wild night of Dungeons and Dragons and Star Trek movies," he teased. But I knew better than that. Atticus' circle of friends was an interesting mix of kids, and they did more than play card games and watch movies. I was glad he had plans for the night as well.

We stood there silently while all around us people were hugging and crying and laughing and congratulating one another. Without thinking, I reached for his hand; he squeezed mine tightly in his grasp.

Maybe it was the prospect of a new beginning at a new school, a shared memory tugging at the corner of our brains. The fact we had grown apart those last couple of years didn't seem to matter now. A single tear rolled down my right cheek. For the moment, Atticus was back.

Chapter Two

That summer, Atticus and I spent nearly every day together, trying to make up for lost time. Abby complained I'd deserted her, and in a way, I guess I did. I loved Abby with all my heart, but my connection with Atticus couldn't be put into words. When I was with Atticus, we talked about real things, not makeup or clothes or which boys liked which girls. We talked about life: our hopes and fears, our plans and dreams. I had missed him sorely. I wasn't ready for the "summer of our re-acquaintance" to end, yet all too quickly we found ourselves traveling the unfamiliar route to our new school.

The public high school was much bigger than our small private grade school. To celebrate our first day, I agreed to go with Atticus into the boys' bathroom. I thought it was silly but Atticus said it was a tradition we couldn't overlook. I liked that we had a tradition, though I wasn't sure if one time in the boys' bathroom at St. Mary's by the Shore qualified it as such. But in we went, giggling the whole time, until Atticus grew very quiet and stared at me. Just like that day in kindergarten.

I felt a little weird, so to break the tension I teased him. "Well, are you going to throw up?"

He smiled, more with his eyes than his mouth. Those

beautiful blue eyes that never failed to take my breath away.

"I love you, Kathleen. I think I have since the first day we met."

Okay, okay. Deep breath. This is Atticus. It's going to be fine. He's your best friend and you love him, too.

"Of course you do. I am quite lovable." I punched his arm in a buddy-like manner, hoping my voice sounded more relaxed than I felt.

He looked at the floor and shook his head. When he looked back up at me, I could see it in his eyes. Exactly what he was trying to say. I didn't need to hear it again. But he said it anyway.

"No, Kathleen, I L-O-V-E you."

I couldn't breathe, I couldn't think. My heart was racing. I wasn't sure why. I willed myself to say *something*. I had always been able to talk to Atticus about anything. I opened my mouth, not sure what would come out.

"I, uh, I..." I stammered as I felt the burn slowly rise to my cheeks.

I had to get out of the boys' bathroom. Why in the world was I even in the boys' bathroom?

Did I love him? Did I L-O-V-E him? I didn't know.

He was waiting on my answer. Waiting for me to say it too. When I didn't, his eyes changed. Nothing else, just his eyes.

I didn't say another word. I just left. And spent the rest of the day pretending I had never been in there.

I somehow managed to avoid him. It was a big school. But there was no getting out of our after-school ritual. We had agreed on where to meet and he would be waiting for me, that much was certain.

The final bell rang and I gathered my books and started a slow trek to the agreed upon meeting place. As I replayed the bathroom scene in my head, I found myself excited to see him. My pace quickened as I summoned up the courage to meet this new Atticus, revealed to me in the boys' bathroom with three simple words.

He'd just caught me by surprise and I needed a little time to digest what he had said. Atticus would understand that. He knew me. As I neared the corner, my eyes scanned each of the intersecting blocks for sight of him. He wasn't there.

The shock of it caught me by surprise. I started to won-der. On the first day of kindergarten, I found my best friend. On the first day of high school, had I lost him?

I walked home alone, dragging out each step, hoping to hear the rhythmic sound of his wheels on the pavement gen-tly informing me that all was well. He wouldn't take my calls or respond to my texts. I spent the rest of the day in my room going over every detail of that now all-important five minutes of my life. He must have felt awful. To tell someone you love them and have them not be able to do much more than joke or stutter. I hadn't meant to hurt him, and know-ing that I did made me hurt for him. I cried myself to sleep, wanting nothing more than to wake up and find it had all been a bad dream.

You can imagine my surprise when Atticus showed up at my front door the next morning, prompt as ever, ready to go school. I tried searching those blue eyes for some speck of anger or hurt or disappointment. Some clue as to which Atti-cus had shown up. He just smiled and said, "Hi Katie," his only concession to his feelings, and in a sense, my own.

As soon as we left the house, I tried to find the right words to explain how I was feeling, even though I didn't know myself. Atticus didn't give me a chance.

"About yesterday," he started, and I could tell this was even harder for him than his admission in the bathroom.

I wanted to make it easier, for both of us. We'd never been awkward in conversation.

"Don't worry about it," I interrupted, desperate not to re-visit feelings the moment resurfaced, as unfair as that might be.

But Atticus wouldn't be put off.

"I'm sorry," he continued. "I didn't mean to put you on the spot. I didn't even know I was going to say that. It just sort of came out. Caught me by surprise too, if you can be-lieve that."

I wasn't sure what to believe, and I wasn't sure what to say. I was hoping he had more to add, because I wasn't ready to speak. Thankfully, he continued.

"We had such a great summer together. I think maybe this whole high school thing is freaking me out a little, and yesterday, I don't know, I felt afraid I might lose you here.

That was a scary feeling. Terrifying actually. And it made me think how much you meant to me. Does that even make any sense?"

I nodded rapidly, hoping to convey that I completely understood. It made sense that out of the protective cocoon of St. Mary's, we all were probably feeling a little overwhelmed and unsure, perhaps Atticus more than most. To be honest, I was sort of excited about the change of scenery, and I thought Atticus was as well because he never mentioned one word of apprehension to me that summer. I was a little sad that I hadn't picked up on it.

I guess Atticus was telling me he got caught up in the moment. So did that mean he actually didn't L-O-V-E me? I wasn't about to ask. I just wanted to be past it.

But the question hung between us, gaining momentum as we made our way closer to school, even if our own pace had slowed considerably.

It was apparent my nodding was not a sufficient enough response for Atticus and he patiently waited for a reply.

Even though his explanation made sense, I felt as if I was right back there in the bathroom, still tongue-tied and looking for a way out. But there was no way out and I said the first thing that popped into my head, which it turns out, made perfect sense because it was the truth.

"It scared me, Atticus, to hear you say that. I don't know if I'm ready for that, you know?"

He thought for a minute, which seemed like an eternity. Atticus knew I hadn't so much as kissed a boy yet. He knew because if I had done anything like that, no matter how far apart we'd grown in junior high, he still would have been the first to know. While many of my girlfriends could rattle off a short list of "relationships", I carefully worked my way through a fairly chaste adolescence. Sure, the idea of a boyfriend was exciting to me, but the reality was a little too daunting, so I experienced blossoming romance and everything that it entailed vicariously, and it suited me just fine.

Finally, he spoke. "Yeah, I don't think I am either."

And that, as they say, was that.

From that day forward, freshman year was a bit of a blur. We were far too busy adjusting to all of the changes to dwell on that five-minute interlude in our lives. We remained good friends, but our incredibly hectic schedules meant we spent less and less time together. I joined the French club and student newspaper and Atticus spent his afternoons involved in student government and band. We both made new friends.

Sometimes we found ourselves together at a school function or a party, and we communicated often via text, but by the end of freshman year, I was missing him more than I realized. I looked forward to summer vacation. Atticus and I always had the best summers together. But I had a nagging suspicion this one would be different.

One year of high school down, three more long years to go. As our various activities wound down, Atticus and I resumed our walks home during those last frenetic weeks spent studying for finals and cramming in last minute term papers. We just sort of naturally fell back into our old routine. Like breathing. So I was surprised, on the last day of school, when Atticus mentioned his summer plans. He'd known for a while and never said a word, letting me ramble on and on about a summer that revolved around the two of us together.

It seems that Atticus Primble had a job.

His uncle on his mother's side was an architect and Atticus had always been fascinated by the process of putting a building together. Even as a young boy he would create these elaborate structures out of the simplest of blocks, always promising to build me the most beautiful house in the neighborhood. All I ever asked was for him to make a house for my Barbies, and Atticus did. I was the envy of all the other little girls at Saint Mary by the Shore.

Atticus was going to work in his uncle's office a few days a week, running errands, filing and most importantly, managing the "large format printer." He said these words with such authority it made me want to laugh but I didn't have the heart. He was pretty excited about it. He said he was saving up his money to buy a new computer, one he could run CAD on, whatever that was.

I pretended to be happy for him, but he could tell I was a little surprised by his announcement.

"It's not every day. We'll still get to see some movies and

go to the pool. Maybe you could get a job too."

I was only 15. I'd be working for the rest of my life. I still wanted to enjoy my summer—with Atticus. How could he desert me? But I couldn't be angry with him. He was genuinely excited.

"Maybe you could meet me some days for lunch," he offered.

For pretty much our whole lives we had spent entire summers together, unhappily separating when our families snuck in a vacation here and there during what we perceived as "Kathleen and Atticus time." I knew he would miss me too.

"Okay, we can meet for lunch, but only if it's your treat, Mr. Large Format Printer Manager," I giggled.

This time when Atticus smiled back at me the most amazing thing happened. I fell in love with him.

I know, I know, it sounds ridiculous. Given all the time I'd spent with Atticus over the years, and all the things we'd shared, it seems an odd moment for me to make that realization. I don't know what it was. I just remember feeling it so clearly. Something changed in him that first year of high school and I wasn't around much to see it. I couldn't quite put my finger on it, but it excited me.

That summer turned out to be the best we'd ever had.

Atticus sensed a difference in me but I didn't dare expose my heart to him. We went to the movies on Tuesdays and the pool on Thursdays and met for lunch on the days he worked - Monday, Wednesday and Friday. Always his treat. Like a date.

And then, the *kiss*.

Oh.My.God. This is so romantic! You are going to die!

We were at the pool. It was really warm, but late in the day, and the sun was beginning to set. Most everyone had gone home already as dinnertime loomed. There we were, just like we'd been a thousand times before.

We were sitting on the pool's ledge, talking about Atticus' job, which seemed to consume an inordinate amount of our conversation that summer. I didn't mind. Atticus was so happy. And he was different somehow. He seemed older to me. The responsibility his uncle had placed in him had clearly left its mark.

For some reason the conversation lagged, an emerging

nuance to our normally constant chatter, a lull asking to be filled, and neither of us quite sure how to satisfy it. I found myself staring into those wonderfully blue eyes once more, eyes that seemed more knowing now, more confident. Eyes that were getting closer and closer to mine until I could feel Atticus' warm breath on my lips.

I closed my eyes because I read somewhere you were supposed to close your eyes in moments like this. My heart was racing so fast I was afraid he would see the movement against the thin material of my wet bathing suit and know how nervous I was. And then, magic. *Really!* His lips touched mine and everything inside of me exploded. That's the only way I can explain it. If I were a balloon I would have popped.

He pulled away slowly, uncertainty about the prudence of his actions etched on his face. It was my first kiss. I didn't know if the rumblings in my belly were butterflies or hunger pangs, but I felt like I needed to eat. And that made me think of a snack time long time ago when there was a different question to be answered. "Will you be my friend?" Atticus had asked me on that very first day of kindergarten. The nuns had interrupted us before I could respond. Now a new question with a new response and all the time in the world to say it. I didn't need any more time. I knew exactly what to say.

"I love you too, Atticus. I have since the day we met."

Chapter Three

Sophomore year, Atticus and I settled back into our abandoned junior high routine, albeit with a new twist. In art class, surrounded by color, I would often drift off trying to decide if his eyes were closer in shade to dodger blue or steel blue. On my way to third period, I would be sure to wait at the first floor elevator so I could steal a quick hello before Atticus headed to chemistry. Once he brought me a dandelion and I pressed it into an old photo album as carefully as if it had been the rarest of African violets.

Our walks home, when our schedules allowed, became more deliberate, punctuated by the laughter one usually reserves for puppy love, and interrupted every few blocks by the need to further explore the sensation of the French kiss.

Atticus and I always had a knack for tuning out the rest of the world when we were together, and now we perfected our indifference to the people around us. At first, no one detected much of a change in our relationship, though I sometimes found my friends cutting their conversations short as I approached. We barely noticed it ourselves, except for the kissing.

My mom was the first to say anything.

We have always been fairly close, the two of us a minority in a house full of big, burly Irish men. She liked to think of herself as a "young, hip mom," and therefore probably felt more obligated than most to neatly balance her role as mother and best friend. I wasn't quite sure how to feel when she wore my clothes and chatted up the girls even though they all seemed to find it pretty cool. I just wanted her to be my mother. I already had a best buddy.

Ever since I can remember, if she wanted to talk about something serious, she did it at breakfast, on Saturday, when my dad and the boys went out for their morning ritual of male bonding. I guess she and I were girl bonding. It's how I learned about my period, and sex, the loss of my beloved hamster, and the death of my even more beloved grandmother. And so, one Saturday morning, as she was reading the paper and having her second cup of coffee and I was enjoying my second bowl of Capn' Crunch, she pounced. Well, that's what it felt like.

"I see you and Atticus are back up to your old tricks," she commented without ever lifting her eyes from the newspaper.

"We had a good summer," was all I would offer.

My mom loved Atticus. And my brothers, knuckleheads that they were, loved him even more. Which made me love them even more. In fact, my whole family adopted Atticus into its womb as if he had been born a Kearney. Capturing their staunchly Irish hearts was no small feat for a boy of English ancestry without a single athletic bone in his body.

"You seem different," she ventured.

I refused to take the bait.

"I like my classes better this year."

My mother would not be dissuaded.

"I heard that Sara has gotten quite serious with Bobby O'Hara," she continued, her eyes still fixed on the paper in front of her.

Sometimes grownups, even relatively cool ones like my mom, used the dumbest terms.

"Yeah, they hook up all the time now." I couldn't help but smirk. My mom shifted slightly in her chair, an almost imperceptible break in her composure.

"Oh, yes, I forgot that's what they called it these days." She found her opening.

"Have you hooked up with anyone yet?" Now she looked straight at me, willing me to fold.

"Mooooooom!" I feigned indignant pride like only a teenage girl could. She looked defeated. She had shown her hand too soon. But I knew that my mom was on to me. "Gotta go." I placed my dish in the sink and hurried out of the kitchen before she had a chance to regroup.

I was meeting some friends at the mall in an hour. Our first sophomore dance was coming up in a few weeks and of course, none of us had anything to wear. Even though I didn't care too much about clothes, I liked shopping with the girls. And since I'd be going to the dance with Atticus as my official boyfriend, I figured I should get something special. Yes, that's what he was now. We sort of kept it on the down low. After the dance everyone would know it. I guess I needed to get used to saying it. And people knowing it. For some reason, it made me a little nervous.

As I got ready in my room, I wondered why I had the sense my mom was not happy about this new direction with Atticus.

It was almost 10:30 by the time I got to the mall. It had just opened and the Saturday crowds were still an hour or two away. Abby and my other friend Julia were already there, gabbing away, no doubt talking about Justin Matthews or Tommy Barrett, their major crushes, respectively. Abby waved when she saw me, and Julia leaned in for a kiss when I strode up next to her.

"Caitlin said she'd be a little late so we're meeting her in the food court at noon," Julia informed me matter-of-factly. Caitlin was always a little late and always meeting us in the food court at noon. She never got out of bed before eleven on the weekends.

I shrugged and we walked through the mall, Julia taking the lead with Abby and I bringing up the rear. I still loved our Saturday morning shopping sprees, but I found myself wanting to be with Atticus more than I wanted to shop.

I guess I was spacing out because Abby was calling my name over and over again.

"Kathleen. Kathleen. Kaaaathleeeeeeen!"

"Sorry, I was thinking about..."

"Atticus," she finished for me barely above a whisper, rolling her eyes.

I could feel the color rising from my neck to my cheeks

and checked to see if Julia had overheard. I hadn't intentional-
ly kept our kisses a secret. But I hadn't shared them with anyone either. Abby had shared her secrets with me. I was the
first person she called when, in 8th grade, Timmy Sheridan
shoved his tongue down her throat and she panicked! And
when, in 9th grade, David Russo slipped his hand up her shirt,
and she let him. By then kissing had become old school.

She looked at me, willing me to tell her. I wanted to. I
wanted to participate in this rite of passage, this sharing of
your secrets with your best girlfriend and giggling over the
strange sensations running through your body, carefully dissecting the mechanics of each kiss and the meaning of every
touch. This ritual of womanhood we didn't even understand
but participated in nonetheless.

I couldn't do it. I couldn't tell her about kissing Atticus.
Not quite yet. But almost.

"I guess I have been thinking about him a lot lately, "I
admitted. Julia stopped dead in her tracks and I nearly walked
right into her; obviously, she had superhuman hearing. She
turned to face me. There was no middle ground with Julia.

"Kathleen, you are *not* going to tell us you love him, are
you?"

Love? Who said anything about love? How did Julia jump
all the way to *love*? Was it that obvious?

I stammered weakly, "Of course not," feeling my betrayal
of Atticus so keenly I almost lost my breath. I backtracked a
little, my heart rushing to his defense, "But I think he's kinda
cute. And he makes me laugh. And we have a lot of fun together. "

"Oh come on, you guys have been friends forever, he's
like your brother. It's a little gross that you think he's cute."

"Well, what about you and Tommy? You always said he
was like the brother you never had, and you *kissed* him last
year! That's grosser."

"That was different," said Julia, with her chin tilted up for
effect.

I didn't see how. Abby just nudged her and said, "I think
Atticus is cute, too."

I gave her a silent look of gratitude.

Julia was about to say something else then thought better of it. She instead focused her attention on a little red

dress in the window of her favorite store.

"I'm gonna try that on. You guys coming?" And in she went.

Abby hesitated. We had a minute to ourselves before Julia noticed we hadn't obediently followed her lead.

"I'm going to the dance with Atticus. As his girlfriend," I blurted out. Wow, it felt really good to say.

Abby's face lit up.

"Really? You're so lucky! No one's asked me yet."

That was her reply. No questions. No comments. No funny look. Why had I waited so long to tell her? Now I felt like spilling all of the happiness, all of the confusion, all of the nervousness I had kept inside of me since Atticus and I first kissed.

I glanced into the store. Julia was talking to the salesgirl about the red dress. She caught my eye and motioned for us to come in.

"I kissed him this summer," I whispered to Abby.

"Is he a good kisser?" she asked, giggling.

I wasn't sure. He was the only boy I ever kissed. But I liked kissing him.

"Yes," I said confidently. "It feels really good to kiss him!" I grabbed her hand and pulled her into the store. I needed a dress!

Atticus and I arrived at the dance holding hands. If anyone was surprised about this very public expression of our relationship, they didn't show it. My mom had seemed a little nervous dropping us off. She never brought up the subject of "hooking up" again, but I am pretty certain she knew. Ever since that day at breakfast, she would ask me, out of the blue, if I needed to talk about anything. I would always pretend not to know what she meant.

Honestly, I didn't need to talk about anything. At least not with my mother. I guess you could say that Atticus and I were taking things slowly. We had done a lot of kissing, but not much more. I knew there was more, but we hadn't gone there yet, though we were getting close. Still, my mom was the last person I would talk to about it.

We got something to drink from the cafeteria and headed into the gym to dance. When we got there, the music was pretty loud and the dance floor was already crowded. Atticus and I had danced before, silly little dance parties of two in the privacy of our homes, but now I felt like people were watching us a little too closely. We pretended not to notice. Abby found us and started twirling me around; evidently she was still a big fan of twirling. Personally, all that spinning got me dizzy! We danced like that for a while, then the lights dimmed just a little more and the deejay started to slow things up. Abby disappeared and Atticus and I were left facing each other, contemplating the prospect of our first *slow* dance.

Other couples on the dance floor had already moved closer, their hands clasped, and their bodies fitting together the way bodies are made to do. I started to walk off the dance floor. Atticus grabbed my hand. Apparently he wasn't going anywhere. It was an awkward moment for me and he sensed it. We had never slow danced before, and, more importantly, hadn't quite worked out the mechanics. How did one slow dance with her boyfriend when he was in a wheelchair?

I looked around at the other couples, so effortlessly lost in this moment. I looked back at Atticus.

"Dance with me, Kathleen." He smiled and simply patted his thigh.

Of course.

I climbed into his lap, hooked my arms around his neck, and placed my head on his shoulder. He smelled good. I felt a flutter in my stomach. Yes, he smelled really good. And it felt really good to be dancing my very first slow dance with Atticus Primble.

We had a great time. Atticus and I barely left the dance floor and Abby managed to get Justin Matthews to be her twirling partner for most of the night. Justin rarely danced and Abby had a triumphant look in her eyes when she hugged me goodnight.

As we were waiting for Atticus' mom to pick us up, Sara and Bobby came out of the gym. Sara looked angry and Bobby looked bored. When he saw me, he smiled. Not just a friendly "how are you" smile but a huge "really happy to see you" grin. I think I blushed. He really was cute. Atticus didn't notice, but Sara did. Which seemed to make her even angrier. She pulled Bobby away from our direction, but he shrugged her off and walked over to Atticus and me. He addressed us both but stared straight into my eyes.

"Hey guys. Great music, huh?" he asked.

"Yeah, the band was really good," replied Atticus, almost a little too quickly.

Defeated, Sara came over too.

"Hi Kathleen, hi Atticus. You guys barely left the dance floor all night."

Then she looked directly at me. "You must be tired, Kathleen. Almost seemed like you never got to sit down."

I didn't like the way she said it, what she was implying. As if Atticus couldn't be tired.

Sara hadn't been the friendliest girl over the years, but she had also never been particularly mean, either. This was mean.

"Oh, but didn't you see," I said smugly, "I got to sit for every slow song," and Atticus and I shared a knowing look.

"I guess I was busy paying attention to something else during the slow songs," Sara said sweetly, and looked at Bobby. Bobby just shook his head. It was obvious something wasn't quite right between the two of them. For a minute I had the weirdest feeling it had something to do with me.

Atticus interrupted my thoughts. "My mom's here, let's go."

I turned to say goodbye to Sara and Bobby. I didn't like the way he was looking at me. It reminded me of when he sat down next to me at Sara's party in the 6th grade. I didn't like the way Sara was looking at me, either. When did I get on *her* wrong side?

Atticus gave them both a quick wave and we headed for the door. I don't think Sara and Bobby had as much fun at the dance as we did.

It was a little past 11:30 pm when I walked in the door. My mom was still downstairs.

"So how was it?" she asked, genuinely interested in my night.

I couldn't hide my happiness, and I didn't want to.

"We had a really great time. Danced all night and now I'm really beat. I'm just gonna go to sleep."

I fell asleep as soon as my head hit the pillow and dreamed of Atticus dancing with me, toe to toe, no wheelchair to be found.

Abby called me early Sunday morning. She was talking so fast I probably wouldn't have understood her even if I wasn't still half asleep.

"I've been texting you all morning!" she screamed into the phone. "Why haven't you replied?"

Sure enough my phone was filled with messages from her. Even a few from Julia. Didn't anyone appreciate a good night's sleep anymore? I didn't have time to read them because Abby was talking a mile a minute, but I did notice that Bobby's name appeared more than once.

"Slow down, slow down!" I yelled into the phone. I imagined she was anxious to tell me all of the details of her night with Justin.

Abby took a breath and slowly repeated her last sentence into the phone. "Sara and Bobby broke up at the dance."

She didn't give me a chance to comment on this apparent wrinkle in our high school universe. I was still trying to piece together what could possibly have happened in the ten hours I'd been asleep.

"And the rumor is they broke up because of *you!*"

Me? Me? Did I hear her right?

"Abby, what are you talking about? You know Bobby and I are barely even friends."

I could see Abby shaking her head on the other end of the line. She knew about these things. At least that's what she always told me. Obviously, I was missing an important piece of information.

"Well, apparently Sara didn't like the way he looked at you at the dance. And Julia told me that Bobby told Sara he liked your dress."

He liked my dress? A warm, delicious feeling crept over me like hot fudge over ice cream. I was secretly pleased. Why was I secretly pleased?

"So, he liked my dress. What does that mean?"

"He didn't like Sara's dress," Abby continued knowingly.

Honestly, sometimes girls confused me, even though I was one.

"Abby, you're making a big deal out of nothing. They did

not break up because Bobby liked my dress better than Sara's! It's ridiculous!"

Abby went in for the kill.

"Well, what he actually said was that he liked your dress and thought Sara should dress more like you do."

Yeah, right. Sara, whose closet I would pay money to raid. Good money.

Now I just laughed.

"You almost had me Abby. Nice try!"

"Kathleen, I'm serious." Abby sounded exasperated. "Sara called Jennifer, who called Caitlin, who called Julia, who called me. Sara and Bobby are over and it's all because of you. Bobby's liked you since 6th grade."

So many phone calls in so few hours. I was feeling a little impressed with myself for being the center of such clearly monumental news.

If Bobby had liked me since the 6th grade, he had a funny way of showing it. I mean I knew in 2nd grade boys ignored the girls they liked, but by high school they were usually a little more obvious about it. Especially boys like Bobby. Boys like Bobby knew they could pretty much have any girl they wanted. If Bobby wanted me, I would have known it.

And yet, his behavior at the end of the dance was certainly peculiar. My heart did a little pirouette at the realization—or at least the possibility. Bobby O'Hara likes me! Wow!

"Abby, I gotta go. I'll call you later." I hung up before she had a chance to argue. I needed to be alone for a minute. But the phone rang again as soon as I put it down. It was Julia.

I answered on the first ring. Julia wouldn't be put off. Might as well get it over with.

"Hey Jules," I answered nonchalantly.

"I've been texting you all morning! Why aren't you replying?" Julia sounded annoyed.

Oh jeez, her too?

"Um, it's 10 in the morning. I was still sleeping," I said a bit snarkily, checking my cell phone again out of habit. Yup, a bunch of texts from Julia just as I'd seen earlier. But wait, there was one I hadn't noticed from a number I didn't recognize. I opened it, curious, while Julia rambled on. It was from Bobby. I didn't even know he *had* my cell phone number. A simple "hey what's up, it's bobby."

"So what are you going to do? Are you going to break up with Atticus?" Julia's shrill voice brought me back to the moment. She was never one to beat around the bush.

"Julia, why would I break up with Atticus? I don't like Bobby." I said the words, but I wasn't sure if I believed them. Apparently Julia didn't.

"Kathleeeeeen...*everybody* likes Bobby! Come on, this is so exciting. I mean, God, it's Bobby O'Hara. Do you know what this means?"

I didn't, actually. I was sure Julia was going to tell me.

"If you date Bobby we'll get to go to all the cool parties again."

Ah, yes, the cool parties. I'd sort of been excluded from most of those once I got to high school. It seems my popularity was short-lived. Julia didn't care so much about whether or not I actually liked Bobby. She just saw him as our ticket to the next level of high school society.

"Jules, I am not going to date Bobby. I really like Atticus." It was true. I didn't want to date Bobby. Still, it was nice knowing he might be interested in me.

"But Atticus...," Julia stopped short, took a deep breath, and then said something that shocked me to the core because I could never be sure if the thing that shocked me more was what Julia said, or the fact that a part of me found myself agreeing.

"Kathleen, Atticus can't walk. You're 16 years old. Do you know how much you're going to miss out on with Atticus as your boyfriend?"

I didn't know what to say. In all my years as Atticus' friend, no one had ever been so blunt about his physical limitations—at least not to my face. It was understood that there were things Atticus couldn't do. But it was never discussed. We always managed to work around them.

"Kathleen?" Anyone else might have backed down at my silence. But not Julia.

"Kathleen, I know it's not a nice thing to say, or even think. But you know what I'm saying is true."

There was so much I wanted to say, to scream! I alternated between wanting to hang up and wanting to defend my relationship with Atticus. I found myself doing neither. My heart hurt. It actually hurt.

Julia kept going, perhaps seeing my silence as a form of implied agreement.

"I know you like him, and I know you're friends. But don't you ever wonder about it? His world is always going to be different."

Finally I found my voice, if not my conviction.

"I think I'm going to hang up now and try to forget what you've said."

I hung up. I was shaking. I was angry. Angry at Julia, but also angry at myself. When Atticus and I had been just friends, it was easier to pretend that his being in a wheelchair didn't matter. As much time as we'd spent together growing up, we had also spent a lot of time apart. Since the summer we'd been virtually inseparable, and I came to appreciate the difficulties that Atticus had hidden from me so well for so long. They were becoming my difficulties and that scared me.

A few weeks ago a group of my friends threw an impromptu party at the parking lot behind an old abandoned movie theatre. I was looking forward to going until I remembered it was a gravel lot and Atticus would have trouble maneuvering around. He insisted I go without him, but I didn't want to do that. So we stayed home and watched a movie as Abby texted me the play by play of the party. I felt bad about not being able to go but I didn't say a word to Atticus.

Another time, when I was practicing what I hoped would be my future signature, Mrs. Kathleen Primble, I wondered how many kids we'd have, in the way teenage girls often do in the throes of their first great love. Then I realized that Atticus wouldn't be able to run around in the grass and play with them. And it made me sad.

Julia's words, while harsh, echoed what I had started to feel but would never admit. Being with Atticus wouldn't always be easy. My cell phone beeped again. I welcomed the distraction from my thoughts. Another text message. From Bobby.

It was a simple message, like the first. The only thing unusual about it was its presence on my phone. "hi! it's bobby again. did u have a good time at the dance?"

I started to text back, "yeah, i had fun" and then changed it to "yeah, me and atticus had a lot of fun".

That didn't seem to deter Bobby. Apparently he was free

and ready to move on.

"Wanna meet at the movies this afternoon?"

I knew what he meant, but pretended otherwise. "I'll check with atticus and c if he's free"

"just YOU" came his reply.

Butterflies instantly found their way into my stomach.

Just like that, it hit me. I wanted to meet Bobby at the movies. I didn't know how much until he asked.

I found myself typing "Y – E – S".

I don't know why I hit SEND. I can't believe I did it. Were my feelings for Atticus so easily disregarded? Julia's words floated into my ears.

Bobby's reply was quick.

"great. let's meet at 7 by the main entrance. c u later!"

What had I done? I was barely a few months into going steady with Atticus and I was planning to meet Bobby O'Hara at the movies! I panicked and my guilt got the better of me. I was in the middle of texting Bobby back to say I changed my mind when my phone rang again. It was Atticus.

"Hi!" I answered the phone in my best "nothing is going on out of the ordinary" voice.

"Hi," he replied. His voice sounded warm and cozy, like he had just woken up from a good night's sleep.

"Did you have fun last night?" he asked me lazily.

I smiled.

"It was a good dance. I especially liked the slow dances," I replied, feeling instantly back to my old self. It was nice sitting on his lap, swaying slowly to the music. It felt right. We felt right. I was definitely *not* going to meet Bobby at the movies.

"Yeah, that was my favorite part too," he admitted. "I was thinking maybe we'd hit the movies tonight."

I froze. For an instant I had the irrational thought that Atticus *knew* about Bobby's invitation.

"I'm not in the mood for the movies. Why don't we just hang out at your house? I don't feel like being around a lot of people. Last night was enough for me!"

I knew Atticus preferred being home anyway. Sometimes it was just easier for him not to have to deal with a world that often forgot not everyone had use of their legs. But he never let that stop him from doing what he wanted to do. Or from what I wanted to do, which seemed to matter more to him.

"Okay," he agreed easily. Atticus wasn't a big phone talker. I assumed he was ready to hang up.

"That was weird with Bobby and Sara last night, huh?" he ventured.

It felt odd to hear Atticus say Bobby's name. He obviously hadn't heard the news. The boys' grapevine always worked a little slower than the girls'. Even so, Atticus wasn't even on the boys' grapevine. He couldn't be bothered. He got most of his news from me.

"They broke up last night," I informed Atticus.

"Really?" I could picture his raised eyebrows.

"Well, that's the news from Abby, which she felt the need to tell me at 10:00 in the morning."

Atticus laughed.

"She probably found out he has a crush on you."

Atticus said it so matter-of-factly, as if he hadn't said anything more momentous than "That math test was hard."

I was afraid he would hear the rapid intake of breath on my end as I gasped at his words.

He was waiting for me to say something about his observation. I could feel it through the phone line. He was waiting for me to say the right thing.

I didn't.

"You know, Abby said that too."

"She did?" Atticus sounded surprised. "I was only kidding. Why would she say that?"

Shit. Since when did Atticus kid about stuff like that? Now what? Did I tell him what Abby told me or just laugh it off? I decided to try and change the subject.

"Oh you know Abby. She's always looking for good gossip even when there isn't any! What time should I come over?"

Atticus didn't take the bait.

"If Abby said it, it's probably true. He was acting weird around you."

I continued my efforts to talk about *anything* but Bobby O'Hara.

"Well, I don't really care one way or the other. I'll come over around five, is that okay?"

Atticus seemed to sense my uneasiness about the conversation. He let it go for the moment, and I hoped it was the end of the discussion.

"Okay, see you then."

"Sounds good. I'll see you later." I hung up the phone without giving him a chance to say goodbye. I finished my text to Bobby.

"changed my mind about the movies meeting atticus instead sorry."

I got to Atticus' house a little after five. His mom was working; she was in real estate and often worked weekends, so we ordered a pizza and decided to watch a movie. Atticus seemed on edge but maybe I was projecting because *I* was on edge. I willed myself to just relax.

We watched the movie mostly in silence until my cell phone beeped. Text message. I casually checked to see who it was, partially hoping it was Bobby, and partially dreading it. Abby, Julia and I texted each other constantly. My ever-beeping cell phone always caused my mom to comment on how it was a wonder she ever got through high school without the ability to text her friends, or call them on their cell phones. It was pretty funny the way she said it, like she grew up in the stone-age or something. Honestly though, how *did* she survive without a cell phone?

The message was from Bobby.

"its 7:00. wish we were still meeting. maybe another time?"

I put my phone back in my pocket and continued to watch the movie. I felt Atticus' eyes on me. How could he possibly know?

He shook his head and laughed.

"I swear Abby and Julia can't live without you for an hour. But I guess neither can I."

He said it so sweetly. At first I felt relieved that he didn't suspect who the message was from. Then I felt guilty because he didn't suspect who the message was from. I put my head on his shoulder.

"I love you, Atticus." I meant it. I loved him. I knew I had to figure the Bobby thing out, but not just then. Just then I was enjoying being with my boyfriend, watching a movie.

I never replied to Bobby's last text. I didn't know what to say. But the more I thought about it, the more I wanted to go on a date with Bobby O'Hara. Atticus was my first boy-friend. And I did love him. Even so, I began to think about what Julia had said. Not about the difficulties of being with Atticus. I refused to let myself go there. We'd managed so far. But she was right that being with Bobby O'Hara opened up that rarified level of coolness that only the privileged few got to be part of. It was a tempting proposition for a girl like me, who'd always hovered between not quite geeky and not quite cool. I thought it might be fun to see what it was like. It also didn't hurt that Bobby was incredibly cute. Everyone had a crush on Bobby. One problem though: I really liked having Atticus as my boyfriend.

That Monday at school things went from bad to worse. It seemed like I bumped into Bobby almost everywhere I went. I did my best to avoid talking to him. I was honestly afraid of what I might say.

Bumping into Bobby wasn't nearly as bad as bumping in-to Sara. Sara, it seems, was not happy at all about the events of the weekend and was determined to let me and everyone else know it. Avoiding Sara wasn't possible. We had three classes together, and the same lunch period.

I could feel her cold stare all through history. During French, it sent a chill up my spine. By the time we got to sci-ence I felt frozen, barely able to focus on a single word the teacher said, which was obvious when my name was called three times and I didn't even know it. I could feel Sara's qui-et satisfaction at my expense.

Lunch was brutal. At the beginning of the year I remem-bered being happy about sitting at Sara's table—even if it was down at the other end. Now I dreaded it.

I tried to convince Abby to skip lunch and go to the li-brary but it was chili day, and she loved chili. On the way to the cafeteria, Abby insisted I had nothing to worry about since I didn't do anything wrong. She was right about that. I never tried to get Bobby to like me. I never tried to break him and Sara up. I was innocent! Surely, Sara would realize that. If she was going to be mad at anyone it should be Bob-by! Maybe I imagined Sara's anger earlier. I started to feel a little better. Until I saw Sara talking to Bobby and laughing.

I could swear a hush came over the cafeteria as I walked in, just like you see in the movies. Sara's eyes followed me to the table—when they weren't focused on watching Bobby's eyes. Bobby was careful not to look in my direction.

I heard Abby mutter "shit" under her breath. "Is the whole school mad at you?" she asked, the sarcasm dripping from every word.

I gave her a dirty look. The library was looking really good right about now. We sat down in our usual spots. Julia was already there and, being Julia, enjoying the drama immensely, having taken over the drama queen title from Abby.

"Isn't this exciting?" she asked without the slightest bit of acknowledgement that this could quite possibly be the worst day of my life.

Abby nudged her but Julia was undeterred.

"Oh, cool, here comes Sara!"

I really wanted to punch Julia. Did she honestly have any idea what I was going through?

Abby's eyes offered quiet support. And then she nodded to someone behind me.

I felt the blood drain from my face. This is not happening. This is ridiculous. I've done nothing wrong.

Somehow I found the nerve to turn and face her. "Hey," was all I could manage but it got the ball rolling, and it caught Sara off guard.

She composed herself and launched into what appeared to be a well-rehearsed speech. She was nervous. I felt bad for her and that made me feel less bad for myself.

"You can have him, Kathleen. He was a little bummed when we broke up but I think he'll bounce back quick enough. I know you've always liked him. Well, now I'm not in your way. He's all yours."

What was I supposed to say...thank you? But I needed to say *something*. The whole cafeteria was waiting for me to say *something*. Okay, well maybe that was an exaggeration, but it felt that way.

I looked at Abby. I looked at Julia. Out of the corner of my eye I saw Atticus. *Shit!* What was he doing here? This wasn't his lunch period. His eyes locked onto mine and he smiled, giving me courage to say the *something* I was sup-posed to say. I smiled back and waved him over. I turned back to Sara. "I don't like Bobby, at least not like that, and I don't want to go out with him. I'm not sure why you think that, but I'm with Atticus. That's all I have to say about it. Now I'm going to have lunch with my boyfriend."

The words didn't sound like mine. I almost didn't believe I said them out loud. I didn't see the look on Sara's face because I was looking at Atticus, rolling toward me with a perplexed look on his face.

Sara glanced in his direction and it looked like she was going to say something to him. I cut her short with the coldest stare I could muster; she backed down. Messing with me was one thing, but I would not tolerate her dragging Atticus into the middle of it all.

With an audible huff for effect, Sara turned around and marched back down to her end of the table. Atticus rolled his eyes. He had long since abandoned his crush on Sara and found her to be "exasperating." His word, not mine.

"What was that all about?" he asked with mild interest.

"What are you doing here?" I replied ignoring his question.

He looked at me like I had two heads.

"Don't you remember? Mr. Howard wasn't going to be in so he gave us a free period as long as we finished our lab. I told you I would be able to meet you today."

Yes, he had. I totally forgot in the middle of my panic about seeing Sara at lunch.

"Oh yeah, that's right. Sorry, this whole thing with Sara has made me a little nuts."

A blank stare from Atticus. Honestly, I knew he didn't pay much mind to gossip but sometimes I wondered if we really went to the same school! Could the Bobby drama really have flown under his radar, or did he simply choose not to be bothered by it?

I figured I might as well clue him in. I gave him the abbreviated version, leaving out the part where Bobby asked me to the movies and I accepted. I could tell he was getting bored with the whole thing before I was halfway through. That was a good sign. It meant he wasn't worried. It meant he didn't suspect that I might have any interest in Bobby O'Hara.

After that day in the cafeteria, Bobby went back to basically ignoring me. It bothered me a little, but maybe he wasn't used to getting blown off, which is what I kinda did that weekend. Eventually, he and Sara got back together and stayed that way for the rest of sophomore year. The world as we knew it continued to rotate on its axis.

At first, Julia was a little upset that our guaranteed entrée into the upper echelon of cool was snatched away so cruelly, but she managed to start dating one of the boys on the football team and eventually made her way to all the best parties. Atticus and I grew closer and I thought about Bobby less and less. The school year ended uneventfully. For some reason I felt like I dodged a carefully aimed bullet, but I was once again looking forward to another summer with Atticus.

That summer Atticus worked for his uncle again; I really missed him. Abby and Julia both got jobs at the mall. And I, well, my mom, decided it was time for me to get a job of my own. My dad's best friend owned a small bookstore and offered me a part-time job there. I'd always liked books even though I wasn't much of a reader. But the bookstore was kind of a cool old place so I thought I'd give it shot. Thursday, Friday, and Saturday, from 10 to 4.

It was the Saturday morning of my first day and, as usual, mom and I were having breakfast at the kitchen table. My dad was in the yard and the boys were sleeping in. No more bonding rituals for them, sleep had become way more important.

"Nervous about your first day?" my mom asked, trying to sound like she wasn't.

"Not really, I replied. How nerve wracking could working in a little bookstore be?

I could tell there was something else on her mind. My mom didn't always have the best sense of timing, but I guess since our mother-daughter Saturday morning chats had become so infrequent, she took whatever opportunity she could to involve herself in my life.

"So Atticus is working every day this summer." It was a statement not a question. She continued, "With you working too I guess it will be hard to see each other as much as before."

I didn't say anything. She didn't seem to notice and kept going.

"Maybe it's for the best. You two were spending a lot of time together. I think you both could use some time apart."

Where was she going with this? Atticus and I always

spent a lot of time together, even when we weren't dating. After the dance, my mom seemed to accept the change in our relationship. We didn't flaunt it in front of her, and she never asked me about it. Up until now, it was almost as if she preferred to ignore its existence beyond a friendship, and that was fine by me.

I looked at her and shrugged. "Is there something you want to say to me?" I asked, knowing full well my mom had a whole agenda she wished to discuss, and also knowing we weren't likely to get past the first item.

"I think you and Atticus should slow it down a bit, Kathleen, and I think this summer is the perfect opportunity for you to do that."

Wow. That was pretty direct for Mom.

"Don't worry, Mom. I'm fine. We're cool." I started to squirm in my seat a little. I didn't like the way she was looking at me.

Mom wasn't cool. Now that she had opened the door, she decided to walk right through.

"Kathleen, you know I love Atticus. I always have. But you're too young to have a serious boyfriend. You should be having fun with your friends."

Was mom forgetting she dated Dad all through high school?

"I am having fun. You had fun with Dad, didn't you?"

"That was different, Kathleen." She hesitated for a moment. I was hoping she wasn't going to say that times were different back then. My mom and dad weren't *that* old. The look in her eyes gave me a nagging suspicion she was going somewhere else with her comment. I didn't like the uneasy feeling it gave me.

I looked at the clock. It was a little before 9:30.

"I don't want to be late on my first day," I chimed as I jumped out of my seat and headed back upstairs to change.

"Kathleen—" my mom grabbed my arm as I walked past her. I stopped and looked at her face, etched with concern. "I know things are serious with Atticus. You should understand what you're getting into. It's just that Atticus is, well, Atticus is different than other boys. It may not seem like a big deal now, but you're not always going to be 16."

Julia's blunt assessment of Atticus was one thing. She was

easy to dismiss. But my mom's words scared me. I didn't want to be scared. I didn't want to think about a time when I wasn't 16. I just wanted to be with Atticus. The way we'd always been. A surge of emotion welled up inside of me. I moved out of her grasp and looked my mom in the eye.

"You're right, mom, Atticus is different than other boys. That's why I love him."

That wasn't what she wanted to hear.

I couldn't get to the bookstore fast enough.

It turned out my mom was right about my not seeing Atticus as much as I used to, but I knew he was busy at his uncle's. I welcomed the distraction of my new job because it helped me miss him a little less. Most of the time things were pretty quiet but I kept busy organizing displays, restocking the shelves and helping customers find just the perfect book for their kid, niece, husband, friend, grandmother. Even though more and more people were reading on their iPads, Kindles, and other devices, there were still enough of them interested in the printed page, and they totally got into their book selection.

I developed a real appreciation for the written word that summer and am pretty sure I read more books than I had read in my entire life up until that point.

Atticus and I managed to see a few movies, hit the pool on Sundays, and grab lunch every now and again. In many ways, things still continued on at a familiar pace.

As time passed, my mom accepted our relationship as more than friends, though I knew she still had her misgivings. Whether those centered on thinking I was too young to be so serious or Atticus' particular challenges, I wasn't really sure. But she seemed to be the only one in my family that had an issue with it, though I suspect my dad and brothers chose to simply leave those matters to my mom.

Some time in August, I can't remember exactly when, late in the day, Bobby O'Hara decided to buy a book. I looked up and there he was. Grinning at me.

"Hi, can I help you?" Ugh. Did I just ask him if I could help him?

"I need a book," came his brilliant reply.

I laughed. He laughed. Before I knew it we were deep in conversation, with not a single mention of any books. In addition to being over the top cute, Bobby O'Hara was funny and smart. I liked being with him. It was easy.

I don't know how he wound up walking me home. Well, I guess at four o'clock I started to head home and he just followed me. What was I supposed to do? I can't lie; I wanted him to walk me home.

For a long while we didn't talk about anything in particular. But as we got closer to my house, our chatter slowed along with our pace. Bobby grew quiet and I didn't know how to fill the sudden silence.

"I'm sorry about what happened with Sara this year," he blurted out.

I gave him my best "it was nothing" wave and kept walking. He stopped. So I stopped. My stomach was doing giant flips.

"I only got back together with Sara because you didn't go to the movies with me," he explained as if I asked him for a reason. "I felt stupid because you blew me off to be with Atticus."

He was talking about stuff that happened months and months ago. Though to be honest, I hadn't forgotten about the movies either.

"Well, I was flattered that you asked, but it wouldn't have been right. I couldn't do that to Atticus."

He nodded as if he understood.

"To be honest, I am not even sure why I asked you," he said, and when he saw the confused look on my face, he rushed to complete his thought.

"No, no, I wanted to ask you. I mean, it was just crazy of me to do because I literally had just broken up with Sara. And even though I saw you with Atticus at the dance, I wasn't sure how serious you guys were so I figured what the heck, it was worth a shot."

I wasn't sure what to say, so said nothing.

Bobby apparently wasn't feeling the same loss for words.

"I was jealous when you guys were slow dancing," he continued.

He said it so matter-of-factly I thought I surely must have misunderstood.

"Jealous of what?" I asked, because I seriously couldn't imagine Bobby being jealous of anyone.

"Jealous of Atticus," came his reply. He seemed as surprised as I was. "Because he was dancing with you. You looked really beautiful that night in that blue dress."

I felt my face flush. He remembered I had on a blue dress. Maybe it was true what Abby had said the morning after the dance about Bobby liking what I wore.

"Sara and I fought about it. It's why we broke up."

I felt a little like a priest hearing his confession. Why was he telling me all this? I didn't want to talk about the reason they broke up.

"Even if you were mad about the movies, you must have still liked Sara to get back together." It was a question as much a statement.

Bobby shrugged.

"I was used to Sara," was all he had to say about that.

It was an odd thing to say, and it made me wonder if I was just 'used' to Atticus?

Our walk was nearing its end, but I didn't want our conversation to end with it. Fortunately, neither did Bobby.

"I broke up with her last week. For good."

Now that was an interesting development. I remained silent. I was secretly glad he broke up with Sara.

"What's going on with you and Atticus?" He asked it so quietly I almost didn't hear him. "You guys still together?"

I nodded.

He started to walk a little more swiftly then. I matched his rhythm, my eyes glued to the ground.

We didn't say another word until we reached my house.

He looked at me, his hands deep inside his pockets. "So now what?" he asked, with a mischievous tilt of his head.

"Bobby, you can't just expect me to leave Atticus every time you breakup with Sara. It doesn't work like that."

He started to interrupt me but I had more to say.

"I really care about him. A lot. I'm not just used to him. I love him."

Bobby held up his hands as if to say "I got it, I got it" and started back the way we came. I had felt his presence next to me so intensely that I was a little lost when he waved goodbye.

I was willing him to look back and say something, anything. It felt good being with him. I didn't want it to end.

"Wait!" I almost turned around to see if someone else had yelled it.

Bobby looked back at me, surprised, waiting for me to say something else.

I chickened out miserably.

"Thanks for stopping by. It was fun. Next time maybe you'll buy a book."

He smiled at me then, as if he knew what I really wanted to say. Somehow that was enough for him.

"Yeah, maybe next time I will."

I thought about Bobby for the whole week. On Thursday, every time someone came into the bookstore my heart gave a little leap in the hope that it was him.

It was so confusing. I didn't understand why I wanted him to come back. I just knew that I did. And somewhere deep inside, I knew that he would. He made me wait until Saturday. Close to closing.

He walked me home again, slowly, as if we both knew this time was all we had. We talked about nothing and everything, careful not to touch upon our conversation from the week prior. When we got to my house, he saluted me good-bye and was on his way. This time he had an extra bounce in his step. I had an extra bounce in my heart.

The following week, he came by on Friday and then again on Saturday. We never talked about what might be going on between us, but I felt different. When I was with Atticus in between Bobby's visits, I felt on edge, even though he didn't seem to notice anything amiss. I decided not to worry about it for now. I hadn't really done anything wrong, only shared a few walks with a friend. But it was much more than that and I knew when school started again things were bound to become more complicated.

Atticus stopped working the week before summer vacation ended. He said he wanted to spend a few lazy days hanging out with me before the craziness of junior year kicked in. It was nice sharing time with him, just like last summer, when we'd first kissed. It made me feel a little guilty about the walks I'd been taking with Bobby.

I dreaded the end of summer more than I ever had before. Somehow it felt like more than summer was ending.

Chapter Four

The night before the first day of school, I was a bit of a wreck. My mom noticed my jitters during dinner, which I had barely touched. If she had anything to say about it, she kept it to herself. I tried to get to bed early, hoping sleep would save me from my fears, at least for a little while. It didn't work. I hadn't seen Bobby for a week, and other than a handful of text messages to one another, we'd kept our distance, as if the start of the school year signaled a silent agreement that our summer friendship was going on hiatus. I stared at the ceiling. No answers there. I covered my head with my pillow to drown out the voice inside me telling me what I didn't want to hear. It didn't work. I was going to break up with Atticus. The thought made me sad.

My head was still covered by the pillow when my mom knocked on my door.

"Kathleen?" She opened the door and stuck her head in. "Is everything okay?"

I shook my head from side to side still hiding beneath my pillow. If I said a single word, I was going to break down. She came over to my bed and sat, and I remembered how good it felt to believe that my mother could make all my troubles go away. I knew she couldn't fix how I was feeling, but having her there made it better somehow. I crept into her arms and cried. A lot. She ran her hand over my hair and promised me over and over again it would be okay until I finally drifted off to sleep in her warm embrace, convinced she was right.

The next morning when I came down for breakfast, she smiled. I spied a plate of fluffy golden pancakes on the table. A real "feel good" breakfast. Not my usual, grab a granola bar and out the door. My brothers stumbled in, suddenly awakened by the smell of Aunt Jemima's best.

"Wait your turn," my mom admonished. The boys looked at each other like the world had gone slightly mad.

I realized I was starving. I sat down, served myself four pancakes, loaded them up with butter and syrup and wolfed them down. My brothers devoured the remaining stack in record time and asked for seconds, which my mom had already started making.

Four was enough for me. My full belly seemed to alleviate the butterflies that had been fluttering there when I woke up. I was still feeling nervous but was excited to get the new year started.

Although I hadn't shared all of the details with her the night before, my mom had noticed the ever increasing presence of Bobby on my walks home from work and correctly guessed he figured prominently in my dilemma. When the doorbell rang and in rolled Atticus, she tossed a concerned look in my direction, but I actually warmed at the sight of him. Something felt right about Atticus picking me up for our first day of school.

I looked at my mom and smiled.

"Thanks for the pancakes. They really made a difference."

She nodded to me, said hello to Atticus and rushed us out the door.

"Get going, guys. You don't want to be late for your first day of school," she said, shooing us like two little chicks.

We made our way to school quietly, hand in hand, each lost in our own thoughts. A comfortable silence for which I found myself grateful as I wasn't a morning person.

The first day was always special for us. It made me sad to think that next year at this time things could be different. In my heart I knew they would be different. I was thinking about Bobby way too much to be Atticus' girlfriend. I would find a way to tell him—but not on the first day of school. At least we could have this last one.

We entered the auditorium for a junior class assembly. Every year the juniors were treated to a first-day scare tactic session to impress upon them the importance of this next step in their education. College visits, SAT prep, career choices—*this* was the make or break year and they wanted to make sure we knew it.

Of course assembly meant bumping into all the people I wasn't quite ready to see—okay, maybe just two people—Sara and Bobby. I hadn't seen Sara all summer. Her family usually went to Cape Cod for a month, which I realized coincided with Bobby's visits to the bookstore.

Atticus noticed my eyes searching the crowds.

"I don't think Abby or Julia is here yet," he said wrongly assuming the destination of my sideways glances.

We continued down the main aisle to the front seating area where special spaces for wheelchair access were left next to some of the regular seating. As I walked next to Atticus, it struck me how I really didn't like sitting all the way up front. Never had.

We situated ourselves and waited for the assembly to begin. I heard Sara's voice behind us, but willed myself not to turn around and look. She was talking to someone, sweetly. At first she was too far away for me to understand what she was saying. As she moved closer, it became obvious.

"I missed you so much while I was at the Cape. I think next year you should come with us for a week."

"Um, yeah, that might be cool." His voice froze my heart. She was talking to Bobby.

"Anyway, are we meeting with everyone at the diner after school? Or do you want to come back to my house? My mom won't be home until five."

Didn't they break up? He *told* me they broke up. They didn't sound broken up.

Atticus started to ask me something and I actually shushed him. I needed to hear the rest of the conversation. He looked at me, puzzled, oblivious to the exchange behind us.

Thankfully, at just that moment our principal, Mr. Jackson, came onto the stage and I pointed, making it seem as if my shush was related. I cursed the coincidence. I strained to hear Bobby's reply, but all I could hear was Mr. Jackson's booming voice. Would Bobby go to the diner? Or would he go to Sara's?

I thought about our walks home that summer, and the way he looked at me. Looks that made me almost break up with Atticus. I felt really stupid thinking that Bobby would actually have been interested in me. He was just biding time until Sara got back.

When the assembly ended, I did my best to avoid eye contact with Bobby. He seemed to be doing his best to do the opposite. I gave in. And he gave me one of those looks. Sara didn't see it. Atticus didn't see it. It was like one of the movie stares—when everyone else was frozen in time except the two main characters secretly in love.

"Come on Bobby." Sara's voice broke the spell and I looked away.

We left the auditorium and headed for our homerooms. Today was a half day. We would listen to announcements, review school rules, get our schedules, fill out paperwork— and catch up on summer gossip.

Not a single person mentioned the breakup of Sara and Bobby. Big news like that would never be kept quiet. Why did Bobby lie to me?

The end of the day bell rang and everyone rushed outside to enjoy the warm weather. Bobby and Sara were nowhere to be found, which annoyed me tremendously. I checked my phone to see if I missed any texts from him but his name was noticeably absent from my new messages. Abby asked if I was going to the diner with everyone else. The thought sent a curious tingle up my spine. Atticus was headed to work for the afternoon and planned to eat lunch with his uncle. The diner would give me a chance to see what Bobby decided, so off Abby and I went.

Julia joined us on the way; we walked the five blocks there, talking excitedly about the new Starbucks that was opening a few streets away. The diner was already packed when we got there and we had to take a seat at the counter. I casually glanced around to see if Bobby and Sara had made it. I didn't want to think of them alone at Sara's house.

They weren't there. I must have frowned because Abby noticed my expression and asked me what was wrong. I didn't want to say anything in front of Julia so I just shrugged and said I missed Atticus. Julia rolled her eyes. She never mentioned the whole "Atticus is different" thing again, but she made it clear in other ways she wasn't a fan of the relationship. Our friendship had suffered a bit as a result, though we still managed to remain in each other's lives. I'd known her for a long time and I guess I was still hoping she'd come around and see Atticus as I did.

Abby never wavered in her support. I think she worried about us though. The more time she spent with me and Atticus, the more she saw the difficulties we faced—or that Atticus faced—and I faced as a result. Sometimes the littlest things turned into the most challenging obstacles. Atticus often said that if everyone was forced to spend a single day in a wheelchair, it would help make things easier for him. It wasn't that most people were purposely thoughtless or mean, they just couldn't understand. Even something as simple as an incline being a few degrees off, something you or I would never notice, changed the experience for someone in a wheelchair.

We ordered lunch and talked about our new classes and new teachers and what we thought junior year would be like. I tried not to let my preoccupation with Sara and Bobby's whereabouts get in the way of my good time with Abby and Julia, but I couldn't help it. I was obsessing over it. What were they doing? Were they talking? Were they kissing? Was he looking at her the way he looked at me? It was making me crazy.

I somehow kept myself involved in what Abby and Julia were saying. Laughing when I was supposed to laugh. Nodding in agreement at the appropriate time. Expressing just the right amount of horror when Julia shared the latest argument with her boyfriend. She put up with a lot to be on the A list, but I think even Julia was getting tired of playing the game. I wondered if it would be like that with Bobby. Part of me felt like Bobby was getting tired of the game—which is why he reached out to me this summer. I liked thinking I could save him somehow—save him from having to be the Bobby O'Hara everyone expected. Super cool. Basketball star. Eventual prom king. Boyfriend of Sara. There was a side to Bobby no one seemed to notice. The side he shared this summer. With me. Maybe I had a special gift to see in people what everyone else managed to miss. Or maybe I just liked feeling needed.

Abby nudged me. I followed her eyes. Sara. Alone. She

looked happy. I figured Bobby would follow but she sat down with her friends and he was nowhere to be found.

My phone beeped. Text message. I expected it to be Atticus saying hello. It was Bobby. I smiled and Abby caught my expression.

"Just Atticus," I lied.

Bobby wanted to meet at the bookstore. I wanted to meet Bobby at the bookstore, if only to find out exactly what was going on. We decided on two o'clock. It gave me enough time to finish lunch with the girls and hopefully avoid any questions.

I was nervous about meeting him—nervous and excited at the same time. He was waiting for me, a big smile on his face as I came into view. I couldn't help but smile back. I didn't care that he lied to me. I didn't care that he was still with Sara. I only cared that he was there waiting for me and still giving me that look. Somehow the rest didn't matter at exactly that moment.

"I didn't think you'd come," he said as I approached.

"Well, I'm here," I said flirting with him a little. It felt good.

He leaned down to give me a peck hello, a recent addition to our relationship during our last few strolls, but I backed away. A kiss didn't feel right at that moment. I needed to know what the deal was.

"I'm sorry," he apologized.

"It's okay. But you need to tell me what's going on."

"With us?" he asked.

Us. I liked the sound of that more than I should. But I refused to get sidetracked by the thought of it.

"No," I replied, ignoring the "us" comment. "What is going on with Sara? I thought you guys broke up. It didn't seem like that today."

He looked away from me then shook his head. I didn't expect him to say what came next.

"I did break up with her, Kathleen. I swear. She just didn't want to hear it. She said we'd take a break in August and then talk. I told her there was nothing to talk about, but she wouldn't listen. When she got back from the Cape, she just pretended like it never happened. She wouldn't listen to me."

I wanted to believe him.

"This morning in assembly you didn't sound broken up. Why did you even sit together?" I wasn't ready to let him off the hook.

"Look, she grabbed my arm and started talking. I wasn't about to cause a scene in the middle of assembly on the first day of school. Why do you think I'm not with her now? I'm with you."

He had a point. He didn't go to the diner with her. He didn't go to her house because she showed up at the diner not long after I got there. And now he was here with me.

"So what about us?" he asked, not giving me a chance to respond to his explanation.

During all of our walks, we had carefully sidestepped any talk of an "us." Now here he was throwing caution to the wind and waiting for an answer.

I wasn't prepared to talk about this just yet with Bobby O'Hara. Suddenly it all seemed too complicated. Breaking up with Atticus. Fighting with Sara. Being Bobby's girlfriend.

I scrunched up my face in response. "I don't know, Bobby. I need some time to sort through it all." It was the truth.

"Can I walk you home?" he asked hoping to extend our time together.

Inside I was screaming *yes, yes, yes,* but the words that came out were "Probably not a good idea."

I felt his eyes on me as I walked away. I thought about turning around but was afraid if I did my resolve would weaken and I would ask him to come with me. So I looked straight ahead and walked home alone. I realized then that Atticus and I never made it to the bathroom that day for our "first day" ritual and shook off the feeling it was a sign.

The first few weeks of junior year were difficult. I felt like I was in a movie, a movie in which I was thoroughly confused and had no hope of a happy ending. Atticus noticed a change in me and got into the bad habit of asking if everything was okay. I never said yes, instead just telling him over and over again not to worry about it, which in hindsight was probably worse. Bobby kept his distance, giving me my requested space and time. Sara, finally admitting to the break up, watched me like a hawk. Abby reminded me daily she was there for me if I needed her. Julia, as was typical, was too involved with her own break up to notice anything else going on around her. My mom served pancakes a little more often, hoping, I guess, the aroma would somehow encourage me to share my burden. I turned away from everyone. I was truly torn.

The thought of leaving Atticus broke my heart. I was sure I still loved him. But I couldn't get Bobby out of my mind. I tried hard to figure out if I liked Bobby or just the idea of him. I read in a magazine that sometimes that happens. I don't think I understood the difference, exactly.

The only thing I knew for sure was that I wasn't being fair to Atticus. I needed to tell him how I was feeling...and fate decided to help things along.

I remember the day clearly. It was a Wednesday in November, a week before the Thanksgiving break. Though Bobby and I did our best to avoid being alone together on a regular basis, we still managed to catch up with one another every now and then, carefully steering clear of the Atticus question looming heavily above our heads. I guess enough was enough because that day Bobby made it obvious he felt he had waited quietly in the wings for far too long. I had to admit, he'd been incredibly patient, and I had been dragging my feet in a misguided effort to prolong a decision one way or the other.

We were walking to free period from science, the only class we had together that year. It was our last class of the day. Something he said made me laugh and he stopped short.

"I really like your laugh," he said giving me what I now referred to as The Look.

I smiled. Bobby liked my laugh. Sometimes it was still hard to believe Bobby liked *me*. That he was waiting for *me*.

Then he pulled me into the gym, which, of course, was empty, because isn't that how it works in the movies? And he kissed me. And I let him. I had to know and this was my chance.

It wasn't just a peck, but a real tongue swirling kiss.

It was pretty good, too. Remember, this assessment is coming from someone who had kissed exactly one boy prior to this, ever. I felt myself analyzing it more than enjoying it. It seemed more experienced and needier than Atticus' kisses. That scared me a little, but it excited me too. My body was telling me something else, like it was chasing a feeling I'd had with Atticus, but not in quite the same way. Bobby's body must have been telling him the same thing because his right hand started fumbling with the buttons on my shirt. I didn't stop him. I didn't help him. But I didn't stop him. It felt good to be kissing Bobby O'Hara in the empty gym. It felt good to be standing up kissing Bobby O'Hara in the empty gym. I didn't want it to stop. But I had to stop. I couldn't do this now. I pulled away.

All I could think about was Atticus—and then suddenly there he was. Staring at me with disbelieving eyes. Eyes I'd never seen so much hurt in before. He shook his head, turned around and left the gym.

For a moment, I was paralyzed with emotion. Bobby hadn't seen him. He just looked down at me and smiled.

"Mmmmmmm, that was nice," he said, unaware of the turmoil in my soul.

I had to go after him. I had to explain somehow. Though unsure of what I was going to say, I wriggled from Bobby's grasp and ran out of the gym, never taking the time to let Bobby know exactly why.

I caught a glimpse of Atticus just as his wheelchair disappeared into the bathroom. I followed him there realizing this meeting was apt to be more public than our first day of school ritual. I shielded my eyes and walked right in.

"Everybody out!" I shouted in fair warning. "Everybody out!"

I heard footsteps shuffle past, and groans of "What is *she* doing in here?" To my relief, the shock of a girl in the boys' bathroom seemed to be enough to clear it out.

"What the hell are you doing, Kathleen?" Atticus shouted, both anger and embarrassment evident in his voice. I wasn't sure if he was talking about my being in the bathroom, or my kissing Bobby.

I had never really seen Atticus this angry. And certainly not at me.

"Atticus, I'm sorry, I'm so sorry." The words came out of my mouth before I had a chance to think about it.

"Sorry? You're sorry? Well, isn't that nice. I'm glad you're sorry. Now get out of here." He couldn't even look at me.

Someone tried to come in and I pushed the door shut. I could hear the murmuring of a crowd gathering outside. Atticus glanced nervously toward the door.

"I know what it looked like, but you need to let me explain!" I said hoping against hope he'd give me a chance to make sense of it somehow.

"Kathleen, it looked like you were kissing Bobby. What could there be to explain? Are you going to tell me that's not what I saw?" He said it calmly, as if he had already resigned himself to the truth I'd been struggling with since the start of school.

I could taste the salty tears now streaming down my face; I looked at the floor, unable to meet his gaze. What could I say? I was kissing Bobby. I shook my head.

"It's just that I needed to see...," my words trailed off. What did I need to see?

His voice softened a little. The anger seemed to fade. Atticus continued.

"Look, I've been feeling you pull away for a while now. We both know it. I wish you could have told me. I wish I had forced you to talk about it more. But I didn't want to admit to myself that something had changed. It wasn't fun to see you with Bobby and find out like that. It hurt. This hurts. But this is not what you want right now. In time I am sure I'll forgive you. But I can't forget what I saw."

The calm in his voice worried me more than his anger. I started to argue, to say he was wrong. He just held up his hand and implored with his eyes for me to stop. This wasn't the place. The crowd outside was getting nosier by the minute. My impulsive behavior had made a spectacle of things, of Atticus, who tried so hard to stay under the radar.

I left him then. I opened the door and walked slowly into the crowd, which grew suddenly quiet and parted for my exit.

I didn't look at anyone, didn't know where I was going. I just needed to be away from there, from that moment. I don't even know when Abby came up next to me and held my hand and walked me home. She didn't ask me any questions, or offer any advice.

I told her Atticus and I broke up. Nothing more. She hugged me at the front door and told me she loved me. I went to my room and cried quietly, somehow keeping my tears from my mom, at least for the night. Bobby sent me a couple of texts. As did Julia. I didn't respond to either. I fell asleep and escaped into a world where Atticus and I were running hand in hand and we were happy.

I woke up the next morning not quite sure of my surroundings. My dreams had been so vivid, so intense, that for a moment, the last place I expected to find myself was in my room.

I jumped in the shower to help bring me back to life, all the while wondering what the day would bring. I had dreamed about Atticus all night. I think it was my way of saying goodbye somehow, of being with him a little longer before the reality of his absence set in.

I tried to get excited about the prospect of dating Bobby. I had already decided I wouldn't do that right away. He would have to be patient just a little while longer. Only Bobby, Atticus and me knew about the kiss. I didn't see the need for anyone to know the reason why Atticus and I broke up. If Bobby really liked me, he would wait. I hoped.

I dried my hair, got dressed and ran down the stairs hoping to make a quick getaway before my mom realized something was wrong.

"See you later," I called out to her as she was bringing a basket of laundry up from the basement. I had tossed and turned all night and by 6:00 am had decided to just get up and start what I knew was going to be a difficult day. I was literally *inches* from the door, granola bar in hand, ready to make my escape.

"Aren't you leaving a little early?" she asked as she neared the landing.

I hesitated in my response. She walked into the living room and glanced out the window.

"Where's Atticus?" It was a simple enough question, and though there were plenty of times we travelled to school separately for one reason or another, today it tore me apart.

"He's not coming," was all I could muster as I choked back a sob.

"Are you okay Kathleen?" came her concerned reply.

I wasn't ready for a long drawn out conversation. I wasn't ready for "I told you so." I wasn't ready for her to tell me it was for the best. And yet, I felt like I owed her some kind of explanation for my obvious distress.

"We broke up yesterday. But I don't want to talk about it, okay?"

"Oh Kathleen, I'm sorry. I know you care about him a lot." That's all she said. I loved my mom but never more than at that moment. I worked hard to keep the tears at bay, but failed. They began streaming down my cheeks.

I opened the front door and said, "I better get going."

She took a step toward me, but then thought better of it. With great restraint, she let me have my space.

"If you need me, I'm here. Have a good day, sweetheart. I love you."

I started to say thank you but the words caught in my throat. I smiled, then nodded, hoping the appreciation and love I felt were somehow reflected in the gesture.

I knew today was going to be tough. What I didn't know was that it would start off in the principal's office.

When I got to homeroom my teacher told me Mr. Jackson had asked to see me before the start of classes. I had never been called to the principal's office before. For a second, I worried something had happened to Atticus and picked up the pace.

When I got there he motioned for me to sit in one of the two chairs across from his desk and cut right to the chase.

"Kathleen, it seems we had a bit of a situation in the boys' bathroom yesterday afternoon. Would you care to explain?"

How could I explain when I was still trying to figure it all out myself?

"I needed to speak to Atticus."

"You needed to speak to Atticus? And you needed to do this in the boys' bathroom?" he asked, raising his eyebrows higher than someone's eyebrows should be able to go.

"Yes. I upset him and I needed to speak to him." It was the truth.

"Ms. Kearney, need I remind you that we have separate bathroom facilities for the boys and girls in this school. And while I have no doubt you needed to speak with Mr. Primble, I cannot condone your doing so in the boys' bathroom. Not only does it show a gross disregard for the privacy of your classmates, but also for the rules of this school. Please see that it never happens again. In light of the fact that you've been a model student up until this point, I am going to let you off with a warning. Should this sort of thing continue, I will be forced to apply an appropriate punishment."

"Thank you, Mr. Jackson. I'm sorry. I wasn't thinking."

"That will be all, Ms. Kearney. You are free to go to your first class."

I walked out of his office relieved that everything was okay with Atticus, and embarrassed by the reminder that my bathroom antics had made the rounds of the school.

I got to my first class early and sat down in the empty classroom. The day had barely started and it didn't look promising. The morning bell rang; the classroom slowly started to fill. Thankfully most of my classmates were still struggling to wake up. They didn't seem to care as much about my bathroom visit as Mr. Jackson did.

My morning classes passed without incident and I was starting to feel a little better about the whole situation. It was a big school; there was always some new drama unfolding. Mine was surely old news by now.

Abby grabbed me for lunch and we walked to the cafeteria, clearly avoiding the one topic I knew she wanted to hear most about. She had texted me earlier in the morning to see if I was okay but the only text I wanted to see was the one I didn't get.

We got our food and sat down apart from everyone else. Julia had since moved to her boyfriend's table. They had broken up and gotten back together so many times I didn't even know from one day to the next what was going on with them. She still had her issues with him but was apparently willing to play the game for a little while longer—well, at least until the junior prom.

I could tell Abby was anxious to hear what had gone on in the bathroom with Atticus because she was fidgeting in her seat.

I jumped right in as if we'd been speaking all along about what had happened the day before.

"So I was thinking. I'd like to go out with Bobby—but I don't think it's the right time, you know, just too soon after Atticus."

Abby didn't miss a beat, thankful to be freed from our earlier silence on the matter. I hadn't shared much with her about my relationship with Bobby, or my doubts about Atticus. As hypocritical as it sounds, it felt disloyal to Atticus to let anyone else know.

"Yeah, I would agree with you there about it being too soon. It *has* only been a day!" she said laughing. "But, more importantly, does Bobby know anything about this?" she asked, her practicality trumping her curiosity.

Bobby. I had completely ignored him since the kiss. He deserved an explanation but I was still working out the details of what that explanation would be.

I looked her in the eye, sorry to have kept her in the dark for so long.

"Well, I think he has an idea," I answered honestly. I was ready to come clean with Abby. "But who knows now as I've pretty much ignored him since Atticus saw us kissing yesterday and..."

She cut me off mid-sentence, leaned in close and whispered, "Wait a minute, back *way* up, you *kissed* Bobby?"

"It was just one kiss, not a big deal." I tried to downplay its importance.

"Is that why you and Atticus broke up?"

I had to think about it. The kiss certainly sped things up, but we broke up more because I *wanted* to kiss Bobby and not necessarily because I *actually* did kiss him. I figured the nuance would be lost on Abby so I just nodded yes to her question.

"Did you want to break up? Why were you in the boys' bathroom? Is Bobby a good kisser? Does Sara know?" Abby's questions came rapidly now, as if her mind was as scrambled as mine.

"Hold on, hold on," I tried to slow her down. I didn't want to relive it but it felt good to be sharing with someone. I trusted Abby.

She listened intently, her eyes wide with surprise. I told her about my late summer walks with Bobby, my feelings about Atticus, my feelings about Bobby, my plan to break up with Atticus, and the *kiss*. She was especially interested in the kiss.

"You didn't say whether or not Bobby is a good kisser. He looks like a good kisser!"

"Yes, he's a good kisser," I admitted, "but..."

"But what, but what?" hissed Abby.

"But Atticus is a better kisser," I admitted, proud for Atticus that it was true. Atticus Primble was a much better kisser than Bobby O'Hara. I thought about his soft lips and his slow kisses and it made me smile.

"Really?" Abby seemed surprised, as if his inability to walk might somehow impact his ability to kiss.

I just laughed. It always surprised me how misunderstood Atticus often was just because he happened to be in a wheelchair. It made me sad to think not everyone was able to appreciate him simply for the person he was inside. Abby wasn't being mean, she just didn't get it.

"Really," I assured her. "I am going to miss his kisses."

I knew I would. I knew I would miss everything about being with Atticus. But I also knew, for the moment, it was time for me to move on.

I didn't speak with Atticus for the remainder of the week. We did a good job of avoiding each other. It was strange not having him in my life, empty almost. I didn't expect him to completely disappear, but that was how he needed to deal with our break-up and I did my best to respect it. As much as it hurt, I believed it had been for the best.

Even so, I asked Bobby to give me a few days to get my head straight, which he thankfully did, waiting until the Saturday after Thanksgiving before reaching out to me over the phone.

When I saw his name on my caller ID first thing in the morning, I smiled.

"Hi Kathleen, what's going on?" The cadence of his words sounded awkward. He was nervous. I realized I was too. By then everyone in the school knew Atticus and I had broken up, but Bobby still didn't know what I was going to do about him and me.

"Not much. I'm working at the bookstore today, but that's about it." Mentioning the bookstore seemed to ease the tension.

"Want me to meet you at closing?" I could hear the smile in his voice.

"Sure, that would be great!" I hoped he could hear the smile in my voice, too. I know it had only been a little over a week since Atticus had ended things, but Bobby and I had been moving toward this moment for months now, and I was ready to see how it would all play out.

"Maybe we could grab a pizza or something on the way

home," he suggested, his confidence returning.

"Okay, stop by around five. I need to close up the store. You can help. We should be ready to go by 5:30."

"You gonna pay me?" he asked.

"No, and I'm not paying for the pizza, either!" I replied, flirting with him. It felt good. Even though I was missing Atticus, I didn't want to be sad anymore.

"Okay," he laughed, "my treat for both. See ya at 5."

So much for taking it slowly. I hung up the phone, trying to decide what I felt. I was looking forward to my date with Bobby, if that's what it was. But I was thinking about Atticus too. This was the first Saturday after Thanksgiving that we wouldn't be having our traditional "Kathleen and Atticus post-Turkey Day Celebration" for as long as I could remember.

I got to the bookstore at 9:30. I was now responsible for opening and closing, though the owner rarely left me by myself. I organized some of the new books and made sure we had extra copies on the shelves of the more popular titles just in case we experienced a post-Thanksgiving Christmas gift shopping frenzy for the New York Times best sellers. I unlocked the door promptly at 10, and in came Atticus.

Seriously, was life trying to mess with my head along with my heart?

"Hi," I said, trying to hide my surprise.

"Hey," he replied, as if I should have been expecting him.

"It's the Saturday after Thanksgiving," he said, knowing I would understand exactly what he meant.

"I know." I started to wonder why he came and I didn't like where my wondering led.

"I thought maybe we could do something after you got off work, just to talk. We haven't really talked since you stalked me in the bathroom." He smiled, trying to make light of that uncomfortable moment.

This was totally unexpected. I started to regret my date with Bobby. Should I tell Atticus? Should I just say I had other plans? Should I say I wasn't ready to talk?

Atticus sensed my hesitation. He knew me too well. He graciously let me off the hook.

"I guess I should have asked you a little sooner, huh?"

"Sorry. I can change my plans though. It's not a big deal." I meant it. I would have changed my plans with Bobby to talk to Atticus. We needed to talk.

He shook his head. "Maybe another time." And out the door he went.

The day dragged on. I felt bad about what happened with Atticus, but I was looking forward to spending some time with Bobby. When he walked in at 5:00 I literally jumped out of my seat.

"Hi! I'm starving!" Yes, that was the first thing I said. Well, I *was* hungry.

"Well, I only have $20 on me so I hope you're not too hungry," Bobby teased.

I gestured to the clutter of books scattered all around the reading tables. "Come on, help me with these books. We need to put them back where they belong."

We straightened up and were ready to leave by 5:15.

There were a few pizza places in town, but Bobby was driving now and I asked if we could go someplace away from the regular crowd. I wasn't ready to bump into people we knew. I wasn't ready for Atticus to find out.

"You're the boss," Bobby said with a small salute and a smile.

I sat quietly collecting my thoughts; Bobby seemed content to let the radio drown out my silence. I noticed that we didn't have the same taste in music and that bothered me a little because music was one of the things Atticus and I loved to share.

When we got to the pizzeria, I made a promise to myself that I would not compare Bobby to Atticus. I was already convinced he would come up short.

We found a single empty table by the door and sat down. Bobby asked me what I wanted. I secretly hoped he liked mushrooms and peppers on his pizza. He did! He went to the counter to place our order, grabbed a couple of sodas, and sat back down.

We looked at each other from across the table. The moment of truth. My stomach was in knots.

"Here we are," he said with a huge grin. "Finally!"

His happiness was contagious. We talked and ate for the next two hours. I remembered why I liked our walks home so much. Bobby was fun to be with. The pizzeria was getting more crowded and when the owner came by for a third time to ask us if we needed anything else, we got the hint and made our way back to the car.

It was still early and I wondered if he'd take me home. I didn't want to go home. Apparently, neither did Bobby.

"I've got an idea. You game?" he asked.

"Sure, where we going?"

"It's a secret," was all he said.

I was afraid to ask anything more.

This time our ride was full of conversation. I wasn't even paying attention to where we were going and was happily surprised when we ended up at an arcade I had never been to. Although Atticus and I went out, we usually spent our time together at his house or mine. I really didn't mind, but I caught myself wishing we had done more.

As we moved easily around the arcade, I couldn't help but notice how difficult some of it would have been for Atticus to navigate. I did my best to push thoughts of Atticus out of my head.

Bobby was no match for me at skee ball, but he beat me pretty badly at hoops. We managed to hit every pinball machine they had and Bobby tilted almost every one. I think he did it on purpose just to make me laugh. We got ice cream and rode the virtual coaster, in that order which I do *not* recommend, and redeemed our prize tickets for goofy sunglasses.

It was getting close to 10 and I'd had a long day. I did my best to suppress my yawns but I was fading fast.

"Ready to go?" Bobby asked.

I nodded, too tired to make a sound.

I fell asleep on the ride home and didn't wake up until we were in front of my house. I felt a little silly, but Bobby told me not to worry about it and teased that I didn't snore too loudly.

He leaned in to give me a kiss. I closed my eyes and let him, kissed him back, and sort of melted into him. It was a nice kiss. I had never kissed in a car before. It seemed like a whole new world was opening up to me. It was different than kissing Atticus. I couldn't help but think that. Just like that day in the gym, it was more urgent somehow, like he was in a hurry to get somewhere else.

I'd always felt safe with Atticus. This felt a little dangerous. I pulled away slowly, hoping he wouldn't notice my sudden trepidation.

"Thank you. I had a nice time." I meant it.

"Me too," Bobby said, with a wide smile. He had beautiful teeth. Still grinning, he continued, "I have a big history test on Monday. Want to help me study tomorrow?"

Tomorrow? He wanted to see me again tomorrow? I thought about Atticus stopping by the bookstore and wanting to talk. After he left I had decided I would call him on Sunday to see if he wanted to meet at the park. I hedged my bets with Bobby.

"Can I call you and let you know? I sort of made some plans already." Sure it was a bit of a lie, but I didn't owe him an explanation. This was only our first real date. Luckily, he didn't expect one.

"That's cool. I guess I'll talk to you tomorrow then." He leaned in for another kiss. This one was more of a peck, a little dismissive even. Now I wondered if he was upset with me.

"Good night," I said as I got out of the car. He watched me walk to my front door. When I opened it, he beeped and waved.

My mom was sitting in the living room, watching the news alone. My dad was an early riser and was usually in bed by 10. She glanced at the clock. I wasn't past my curfew but I know she was thinking I'd had a long day. She was right. I was exhausted.

"How was your date with Bobby?" she asked as conversationally as she could. When I told her that morning I was meeting Bobby after work she seemed surprised, but didn't say anything other than to call if I was going to be late.

"It wasn't a date, Mom. We just went out for pizza." I didn't mean to sound so defensive but I guess I did.

"Ah, yes, pizza. Must have been an extra large pie." She laughed at her own joke. I laughed too. We'd been gone way too long for just pizza. I stuck my tongue out at her and headed off to my room.

"I'm really beat, mom. I'll talk to you in the morning."

I collapsed onto my bed and woke to the sound of my cell phone ringing. I rubbed the sleep from my eyes and checked for the time. I must have been pretty tired because it was a few minutes past noon on Sunday. The display on my phone told me it was Bobby calling. I didn't answer. I needed to wake up a little first. I wanted to see Bobby. But I wanted to see Atticus, too. I dialed Atticus' number. He answered on the first ring.

"Hey!" he said. I could hear the pleasure in his voice.

"Busy today?" I asked before I could change my mind.

"Not really. What were you thinking?" It was almost as if nothing had changed, the way we fell into our usual banter.

I looked out my window. The sun was shining, the sky was blue. The perfect fall day.

"How about a walk in Jefferson?" I suggested. Jefferson Park was a few blocks away and it had a long, winding walking path that was neatly paved and mostly level. We'd spent a lot of time there.

"Sure! I'll swing by around one if that's good. We can grab a hot dog at Fred's," Atticus suggested.

Fred's was the hot dog truck permanently stationed in the park no matter what the weather. Atticus and I grew up eating Fred's hot dogs and listening to his stories. It seems the park was never a dull place to be. In the summer, there was always a long line to get his famous secret recipe "delicacy."

"Okay, see you then." I hung up the phone and stared at the ceiling. I missed Atticus. I missed my best friend. I was glad we were going to take a walk together.

I sent Bobby a quick text. I said I had other plans and would talk to him later. I guess that was enough for him because he didn't send a reply.

I took a quick shower, pulled my hair into a ponytail and went downstairs to wait for Atticus. My mom and dad were sitting at the kitchen table eating lunch.

"You're up early," my dad said, getting more of a kick out of himself than he should.

I'd never known him to sleep later than 7:00 am even on the weekends. He couldn't understand why anyone would want to waste a perfectly good morning sleeping in. My mom said he was like that in high school, too. So unlike my brothers and I who slept late whenever we could.

"I'm going to the park," I said, noncommittally.

"It would be nice if you stayed home once in a while. I feel like we never see you anymore," my dad complained good-naturedly.

"I won't be long," I promised, "and when I get home I'll beat you at Guitar Hero if you want."

He laughed and said, "You're on!" It was the only video game he had ever played and he was hard to beat. But every now and then I pulled out a victory.

I sat down thinking I had successfully diverted their attention away from my park outing. No chance. Not with mom there.

"Are you meeting anyone at the park?" she asked. Her answer didn't come from me. It came from Atticus, rolling right in, just like Atticus always did.

I could see the confusion on my mom's face.

Atticus didn't notice. He barely even noticed my mom and dad were there. I started to think this might have been a bad idea. Atticus seemed a little too happy to see me.

"Hey, Kathleen. You ready to go?"

My dad cleared his throat.

"Oh, hi Mr. and Mrs. Kearney. Really nice day out," said Atticus, acknowledging them but still not looking in their direction.

"Yeah, let's go." I desperately wanted to be away from my mom's now disapproving stare. "See you guys in a little while."

Once at the park, we took our normal route, the one with the fewest bumps, the silence between us a little less comfortable than it used to be. It dawned on me that so much of what we did was planned in advance to accommodate Atticus' situation. It had never bothered me before. Today it stood in stark contrast to the easy, spontaneity of my date with Bobby.

We had only walked about a quarter mile into the park when we came upon an area of the path that had been recently repaired and was blocked off by yellow construction tape. On either side the ground was muddy, making it impossible for Atticus to pass. He looked a little defeated. I was sad for him, for us. There was a time when I looked at Atticus and saw only the future. Lately, I saw obstacles I'd never considered before. I didn't like the way it felt.

It struck me that the blocked pathway became symbolic somehow.

Atticus turned around.

"Oh well, guess we can't go any further," he said as he rolled his wheelchair in the opposite direction.

Was he talking about us, or the pathway?

"We can find another path," I insisted, determined not to let a piece of yellow tape dictate the future for Atticus and me. I realized I was being a bit dramatic, but I felt if we found another path everything would somehow be all right. Atticus misunderstood why I was so driven to find an alternate route through the park.

"It's okay, Kathleen, we can go somewhere else. It's not a big deal." He was always so accepting of his circumstance. I used to be as well. Not this time.

"No, no it's not okay. We have to find another way. We can't just give up."

Atticus was staring at me, perplexed. I felt a rush of color rise to my cheeks. I couldn't control my outburst. It was as if years of giving in to these little obstacles had come to a head at this very spot, and if we couldn't find a way around it, all would be lost for us.

I grabbed Atticus' wheelchair and started pushing it. I never pushed him. He was far too proficient with his wheelchair to ever need my help. But today I needed this. He lifted his hands in mock submission. He wasn't easy to push but I didn't dare give up. I found a new path, one we'd never taken. We didn't know its twists or turns; we didn't know its bumps or boundaries; we didn't know its texture or terrain. It was slow going. Although he felt my struggle, Atticus didn't say a word. He just let me push him.

At the end of path we found a delicate field surrounded by the most beautiful little trees, bursting with autumn color. I knew it would be difficult to push Atticus there but I didn't care. We were getting to the middle of that field if it took every ounce of strength I had.

"We've never been here before," said Atticus, his voice almost a whisper. He could feel it too. The sadness. A quiet longing for all we missed.

I pushed him as far as I could before finally collapsing onto the ground. Atticus helped himself out of his chair and sat next to me. We used to sit for hours, wordless, simply enjoying the prospect of being together, but the quiet made me self-conscious now and I felt compelled to speak.

"How was Thanksgiving at your aunt's this year?" I asked the question, already knowing the answer but we had to start somewhere.

Atticus nodded and rolled his eyes. His aunt was a bit eccentric. She had made it a tradition not to serve a classic Thanksgiving meal. No turkey, no stuffing, no sweet potato pie. Half the time Atticus didn't know what he was eating. Every year he snuck a plate home just so we could examine it in detail and try to figure out what it was, as part of our post-Turkey Day celebration. Some years it was easy. Others, we decided it was best we didn't know.

"I saved a plate, but then when you had plans yesterday, I threw it away," he explained.

"Oh," was all I could say to that.

"Whatever it was, it was pretty awful," he continued, perhaps trying to downplay whatever significance he imagined I read into his actions.

Silence again.

"How was your date with Bobby?" He asked it so matter-of-factly it caught me by surprise. Was he fishing?

I turned to him, not sure how to answer, but in the end the truth seemed to be the best choice.

"It was nice," was all I could manage. I pulled my eyes away from his.

"I'm okay, Kathleen. That's why I wanted to see you today. To tell you that."

He waited for me to say something in response. When I didn't, he continued.

"You are my best friend. You have been since the day we met. I was hurt when I found out about Bobby. It still hurts. But I know you didn't lie to me. I know you didn't want to hurt me. And, for purely selfish reasons, I do not want to lose my best friend. I just thought you should know that."

Wow. It was exactly what I wanted to hear. I could date Bobby and still have Atticus in my life. It should have made me happy. Instead, I felt like I was still losing Atticus somehow.

I smiled at him, staring into those blue eyes, which didn't seem at all sad. Atticus was going to be all right. It was me I was worried about.

Chapter Five

The following week Bobby and I met every day after school. Atticus and I spoke on the phone once or twice but avoided any direct contact. I guess it would take some time to figure out how to dial things back to simply being best friends again given all that had transpired. It didn't help matters that it was all over school that Bobby and I were now a couple.

I was swept into a whole new social existence. Abby benefited as well from some sort of perceived halo effect, and Julia found the gumption to leave her boyfriend once and for all. She didn't need him now. Her association with me was enough to get her invited to all of the coolest parties.

I was less affected by my new social status. I didn't care to meet new people. And while Bobby was actually interesting to spend time with, I thought his friends a little immature and shallow. Sometimes Bobby was like that when he was with them. I recalled Atticus feeling similarly in Junior High. I thought it was him that had been acting poorly but maybe I had changed then as well.

Saturday night, there was a big party planned. I didn't want to go but Bobby was looking forward to it. He really wanted me there with him. Abby and Julia spent most of our lunch periods frantically discussing just the right thing to wear and grilled me on my wardrobe selections for the party. Suffice it to say, they were not pleased with the fact that I hadn't given it a lot of thought. I guess it was odd. I mean, I've been known to shop for days for just the right pair of jeans. I just wasn't into it.

It all seemed a little much for me. Bobby and I had barely been dating a week! Things certainly moved quickly in this next echelon of the social strata.

Atticus and I had years to get to know each other before we started going out. Everything just fell into place and no one really cared that we were dating. With Bobby, our relationship seemed to be everybody's business. People looked at me differently and acted differently around me. I swear sometimes I half expected people to ask me for my autograph! It was almost as if it was too much work being Bobby's girlfriend. Too much to think about. The thought struck me as funny. I am sure Abby and Julia believed it much harder to be Atticus' girlfriend. I didn't see it that way at all.

The party on Saturday started out well. Somehow Ryan Tottenberg managed to secure his house for the evening and I remembered hearing something about his parents and Aspen.

Bobby encouraged me to have my first taste of beer. I didn't like it so I put the glass down. I didn't see the point in drinking something I didn't like. Bobby and I danced and laughed and he introduced me to all of his friends, many of whom were in my classes yet had never given me a passing glance. Now, I was their new best friend.

Of course, Sara was there, looking more beautiful than ever, in just the right jeans and just the right shoes. Perfectly turned out as always. Minus one very important accessory.

Still, she did her best to make Bobby jealous. He truly seemed to only be interested in me and somehow that made me feel more beautiful.

I was feeling especially beautiful when we found an empty bedroom and snuck in to be alone. Bobby's kisses made me feel so alive, so adult. His hands moved over me in places Atticus' had never been, and I was more than happy to let them explore. My body responded in ways that were new to me, though they didn't seem new to Bobby. I started to get that feeling again, excited and afraid at the same time. Excited won out and I cautiously let him lead me into this new world, wondering if I was really ready to go.

Knock. Knock. Knock.

I jumped up, hastily pulling my shirt back on, and trying to figure out when it actually came off.

Bobby seemed unconcerned about the unexpected visitor and casually responded with a "What's up?" Clearly, he had experience in this type of situation. He hadn't even moved from the bed.

"Hey, Bobby, Abby's not feeling well and was looking for Kathleen," came the whispered reply.

My immediate response was to get up and go to my friend, slightly embarrassed that whoever was on the other side of the door knew exactly where to find me.

Bobby reached his hand out to stop me.

"Can't Julia help her?" I did not like what I heard in his voice.

"She asked for Kathleen."

It was all I needed to hear. Annoyed, I pushed Bobby's hand away and went to find my friend.

She was sitting on a couch in the living room, a group of girls huddled around her, affecting mock concern. Who were these people? I chased them all away and Abby looked at me with grateful eyes.

"I think I had a little too much to drink," she muttered, her eyes to the floor.

Abby and I had never been to a party where they served beer. I had the distraction of Bobby to keep me from drinking the night away. With Julia flitting around making sure her ex-boyfriend saw exactly how little she missed him, Abby, I realized, was more or less alone. So she chose the company of a new friend—Budweiser. They did not get along.

"Can we go home?" she asked simply.

Bobby came up behind me.

"I am sure we can find someone who can take her home," he said dismissively.

Perhaps he had been the center of Sara's world, but I wasn't about to abandon a friend for him. I gave him a sharp look, and he quickly found a more suitable alternative, one he knew would be to my liking.

"I haven't had anything to drink. I can take her. Let's go."

As the words came out of his mouth, Bobby looked to me to make sure I was satisfied with his new plan for getting Abby home.

Before we even got to the car, Abby threw up twice. Watching her wretch until she had nothing left inside, and listening to her muffled sobs, tears streaming down her face, made me realize that drinking wasn't all it was cracked up to be, that it wasn't worth the trouble.

Unfazed, Bobby casually commented, "She'll be okay tomorrow. She needs to sleep it off. Come on, let's get her home and get back to the party."

Back to the party? Did he really just say that?

"She is sleeping over my house tonight," I reminded him. There was no way I was going to leave her alone.

Bobby shrugged and said he'd get the car. He hesitated for a moment, then asked, "Do you think she's done being sick? I have my dad's car and..."

I cut him off mid-sentence. I was focused on taking care of my friend and getting her back to my house. "Get the car. I'll get something from the house just in case."

Bobby dropped us off and I barely said good night. Abby was feeling a little better but I still had to help her into my house.

It was still early enough for my mom to be up and I said a silent prayer that she was already reading in bed, pretending not to wait up for me.

The kitchen was empty, so far so good. All clear in the living room, too.

We crept up the steps, my right arm wrapped firmly around Abby's delicate shoulders, squeezing her tight, as if I could will some of my soberness into her.

I saw the light coming from under my mom's bedroom door.

"We're home," I said as casually as I could, and I nudged Abby to remind her to say hello to my mom and dad.

"Hi, Mr. and Mrs. Kearney. Thanks for letting me stay over," she said weakly, managing to be polite even in her queasiness.

We shuffled into my room and Abby collapsed onto my bed. I felt a little guilty thinking about my bed the same way Bobby thought about his dad's car. I too was hoping Abby was done being sick. Maybe I had been a little too hard on him.

I didn't even hear the knock. When my mom walked in I knew there was no hiding the fact that Abby wasn't quite herself.

I braced for my mother's recriminations.

"You're home a little early. Is everything okay?" my mom asked, not jumping to the obvious conclusion, even though her eyes were clearly not looking in my direction.

I sighed and responded honestly, hoping for the best.

"Abby had a little too much to drink. I think it's the first time she ever had beer."

My mom's eyes locked onto Abby sleeping on the bed as if she were a doctor assessing her physical well-being.

"My first time, too. I didn't like it," I added for no particular reason.

"Well, it seems Abby did," my mom replied, the concern evident in her voice.

"She threw up twice before we got here. I think that helped," I offered.

My mom looked at me but didn't say a word. It wasn't the time for a lecture. We both knew it. That would come later.

"Let her sleep. Call me if you need me. We'll talk more in the morning."

She gave me a hug, felt Abby's forehead, and walked out of my room. Sometimes I was surprised by how well she really knew me given the minuscule amount of time I let her into my life. I knew she was disappointed. She knew that stung far worse than any angry tirade ever could.

I lay awake for a long time thinking about Bobby and Abby. I thought about Atticus too, because he had always been my barometer for acceptable behavior. What would Atticus have done? How would he have reacted? I knew the answers before I even asked myself the questions. I smashed my head down into the pillow face first and tried to shake away the comparisons. Bobby was my boyfriend now. I wanted Bobby to be my boyfriend.

That night I dreamed of Atticus, running through a field. He was smiling so widely, his blue eyes sparkling, perfectly matching the cloudless sky. And he was running *away* from me.

Abby was up first, surprisingly alert and not nearly as hung over as I would have expected. Then again, I had no idea what to expect having never quite seen anyone with a hangover.

"You awake?" she grunted in my direction.

I yawned an unconvincing "yes" while stretching my arms above my head and wondering why I felt so incredibly sad.

"Is your mom mad?" she asked, finding her voice.

I knew my mom wasn't mad. It still didn't mean we'd get off easy.

I sat up and looked at Abby. She was a mess.

"Go take a shower. I'll see what we're having for breakfast," I replied, ignoring her question because I didn't know the answer.

Abby didn't move. She hugged her knees, pressing the side of her face down on top of them.

"Thanks for taking care of me. You're a good friend."

She got out of bed moving more like an old man than a 16-year-old girl and paddled off to the bathroom.

I smiled. I knew Abby would have done the same for me. I smiled more when I smelled the scent of cinnamon and maple syrup slowly making its way up to my room. I knew instinctively that meant a serious talk, and a lot of love. I was ready for both.

We sat at the table like two obedient little girls, neither of us daring to utter a single word. My dad was conveniently at the store, and the boys were never up before one these days unless they had a game of some sort, which, thankfully, wasn't the case today. Just the girls. And waffles.

My mom served us and sat down. She'd already had her breakfast and coffee and I was certain she had spent the better part of her morning thinking about exactly what to say.

"How are you feeling, Abby?" she asked, her voice pouring over us as smooth and warm as the maple syrup over our breakfast.

"I'm okay, I guess," answered Abby. "My head hurts and I'm still tired. But I'm okay."

"I spoke with your mother this morning," said my mom. "She is not too happy about the beer, and neither am I."

Abby and I remained silent. It seemed like the best course of action at the moment.

My mom continued. "I drank a lot in high school," came her quiet admission.

My mom drank in high school? I wanted to laugh.

"Too much, actually. One night I was at a party with my friends. My boyfriend was supposed to take me home but he left without me because he was too drunk to remember I needed a ride. I was too drunk to notice he left."

My mom drinking was one thing. My mom "too drunk" was quite another.

"I loved him. We planned to go to college together and get married. He crashed his car into a telephone pole that night and died. I never drank again."

My eyes searched hers. I could see there was much more left unsaid.

She gave each of our hands a squeeze then left us to our waffles and our thoughts.

When Bobby called me later in the day, long after Abby had gone home to deal with her parents version of an appropriate response to her poor judgment, I had already decided not to make a big deal about what I felt was a huge display of insensitivity on his part. Even though he attempted to sound concerned on the phone, it was a little too late for that in my eyes and I wasn't in the mood to talk. I was still thinking about what my mom had told us. I never knew she had a boyfriend other than my dad in high school. I never knew she was in love with someone else. Maybe she understood more about me than I thought. I didn't mention any of it to Bobby. I would have told Atticus everything.

Monday morning lazily made its way through the halls of our high school. Abby and I took our usual route to first period English. She mentioned she was grounded for a week, no visits, no cell phone, no email—hence our inability to further discuss Saturday night's events on Sunday, though she confessed my mom's story did more to convince her of the ills of too much alcohol than seven days of no social life. Well, that and the fact that she absolutely hated the way she felt the next day.

"She never told you about that before?" she asked me, as curious as I to know the details of my mom's newly discovered secret.

I shook my head slowly from left to right, half listening to Abby, half replaying the scene in my mind and trying to remember if she'd ever mentioned another boyfriend.

"I wonder why?" Abby questioned. "Did she tell you anything else after I left?"

"Not a thing," I replied. I had waited the rest of the day to hear more, but that was the last she mentioned of it.

My mom loved to tell the story about how she and my dad met in high school and fell in love, about how she waited two months before agreeing to date him, and about how after college she waited two years before she agreed to marry him. She was a cheerleader. He was on the football team. And they were, of course, king and queen of the prom. There was never mention of another boy, or another life. Never a hint of sadness or regret. I was beginning to think she made it all up just to prove her point. But who would make up a story like that. It would be a little macabre, even for a well-intentioned parent.

"Are you going to ask her about it?" Abby posed.

I shook my head no.

Of course, I wanted to, was dying to, but I felt this unspoken agreement between us, that she would tell me more when the time was right. I was hoping the time would be right soon.

Bobby caught up with me at lunch and we made plans to hang out with his friends after school. It never crossed my mind to share with him what my mother told me. Yet, all day I was hoping to bump into Atticus so we could talk it through.

I noticed in the weeks that followed, before Bobby dropped me off at home, he would take detours to dark, quiet streets, where our kisses goodnight turned into what I started to refer to as grope fests.

It wasn't that I minded the groping. I was interested in exploring the new sensations I experienced the night of the party. I just didn't feel comfortable parked on the street. Even in the dark, I still felt exposed, sitting there in the car with my shirt pushed up to my chin.

Bobby didn't seem to be bothered in the least, and I silently wondered where he and Sara had their groping sessions. A lot of people were convinced they had even done "it" though I never asked him. He certainly kissed like someone who knew what he was doing.

Eventually I expressed my discomfort with the whole car situation.

Bobby didn't miss a beat.

"My parents are going out on Saturday night. Would you be more comfortable in my room?"

I felt like he wasn't just asking me about my comfort level with location. There was more to his question. He looked at me with expectant eyes.

My reply was barely a whisper. "Yes." It was Tuesday.

I counted down the days until Saturday, mentally checking them off in my head. On Friday morning, my stomach felt like it was going to run away from the rest of my body. I was excited but a little terrified, too. I had been alone with Atticus in his bedroom countless times. I knew this wasn't going to be quite the same and I wondered what I had actually agreed to. Was it my imagination or was Bobby looking at me differently? I hadn't told anyone about our plans, not even Abby. Apparently, Bobby felt the need to share.

"Kathleen, are you really going to do it with Bobby tomorrow night?" Abby's accusatory question came through my cell phone like a rocket ship.

"Huh?" I replied, momentarily caught off guard by her tone. It was 7:30 in the morning and although I was dressed and walking out the door, I was still half asleep.

Abby fired away, almost as fast as the first time.

"Julia told me that Anna told her that Sara told Anna that you and Bobby were going to do it Saturday night."

I paused, momentarily confused, and Abby jumped to fill the silence. "Why didn't you tell me? Why did I have to find out from Julia? I felt so stupid not knowing." When I hesitated further, she added, "Where *are* you?"

I tried to replay Abby's words. But the only question I felt I could answer was the last.

"I'm two blocks from school. Meet me at the umbrella tree."

I checked the time on my phone. We would have twenty minutes before first period. More than enough time to give Abby some kind of explanation.

The umbrella tree was where we met whenever there was something urgent to be discussed before the start of the school day. We called it the "umbrella tree" because its lush, wide canopy perched atop a tall, thick trunk, resembled exactly that. Our umbrella tree not only shielded us from the sun on hot summer days and the rain on warm spring mornings, but over the years its broad, leafy branches offered us protection from the world when we needed a quiet place to be, offering a favorite blanket's soft, enveloping embrace.

She was there waiting for me, pacing the already well-worn path in the shaded area beneath.

As I walked towards her, she turned, her eyes full of questions—and hurt.

"I don't understand. Why didn't you tell me?" she asked simply. "You promised."

Yes. We had promised. We had shared so many firsts with one another. First kiss. First feel. First heartbreak. We pinky-promised to share *that* first from the moment we found out what it was, though at the time we cringed at the possibility.

"Nothing's happened," I replied honestly, trying to shrug away her question, trying not to sound as defensive as I felt.

She raised her eyebrows.

"But it's going to, and it's already Friday. You didn't think I'd want to know? How would *you* feel if it were the other way around?"

I looked down at the ground, hiding my eyes from her piercing gaze. Abby would have called me the minute the plans had been made. The two of us would have spent the week plotting out every possible scenario, our emotions straddling somewhere between giddy anticipation and abject terror.

The truth is I didn't want to tell Abby. I didn't want to tell anyone. I didn't want to pour over every detail because I didn't want to think about it. I realized then, that I just wanted it to go away. I didn't want it to happen. I looked up at Abby, not sure what to say.

Abby, true friend that she was, looked into my eyes and came to the same realization.

"Oh, Kathleen," she murmured as she pulled me in close. I nestled my face into her Pert Plus-scented hair, and cried.

"You need to tell Bobby," was all that Abby said.

At the end of the school day Bobby texted me he had some things to do to plan for our date on Saturday and he'd call me later. The multiple happy faces at the end of his message, which usually sent my heart fluttering, irritated me now. I decided to walk home instead of catching the bus. I needed time to think.

I absent-mindedly followed the familiar path I had taken all of my high school years: a route, I recalled sadly, which I rarely trekked alone before this year. Atticus had always been by my side. I imagined him there next to me, allowing me my silence. Knowing intuitively I would open up to him, he would patiently wait for my nerve to kick in.

Lost in my thoughts, I didn't hear the light swoosh of his wheelchair as he pulled alongside me. He touched my arm, smiled, and simply said, "Katie," with his head cocked to the side like a puppy with a question it didn't know how to ask.

We walked and walked, and I was once again reminded of the absolute comfort his quiet presence always brought to my heart.

He uncharacteristically broke the silence.

"I know about Saturday."

I cursed Bobby under my breath, further uneased by his obvious lack of discretion about something I felt was incredibly personal.

Still I said nothing. What was there to say? Particularly to Atticus.

It dawned on me then that there was so much to say. So much I had wanted to say. To Bobby.

I reached for Atticus' hand, squeezed it once, and said, "Thank you."

He held it far longer than he needed to. With a slight nod, he pulled away and left me alone with my thoughts. I dialed Bobby's number.

Bobby surprised me. He was so apologetic for his errant words, so ridiculously committed to making it up to me, that I couldn't help but forgive him. It was the first time I considered he might really love me. Going steady with Bobby O'Hara was one thing. But being loved by Bobby O'Hara, well, that was something my grade school self would have never ever imagined.

We spent that Saturday night talking. About anything and

everything. We lay in his bedroom, tangled up in each other's arms, chatting the night away. Frankly, I wanted to kiss. I wanted to do more than kiss. But it seems I touched on a nerve with Bobby and he wasn't done examining what almost happened between us.

Guess what?

Bobby had *never* done it!

He sheepishly admitted he liked people thinking he had. He never told anyone that he had, but he never corrected them, either. When Sara chose to keep people guessing as well, he decided it was okay to leave things as they were. What harm could there be in that?

Bobby apparently felt a lot of pressure to uphold this image that everyone had of him. He knew it was silly, knew it shouldn't matter. When he started dating me, he felt like he was more himself than he had ever been; he felt I liked him for him, and not because he was Bobby O'Hara.

This was true, of course. But the Bobby O'Hara factor didn't hurt. I didn't tell him that, though.

He went on to say that seeing me with Atticus made him realize what a special person I was. He brought up the night of the dance, my first official public outing with Atticus, and how he watched me dance with him, as if his being in a wheelchair didn't matter.

His exact words: "If you could be with someone like that, I knew you had to be special."

I bristled at the implication that there was something "wrong" with Atticus, but I knew Bobby wasn't trying to be mean. Still, my need to defend Atticus was as strong as ever.

"You know, Bobby, his wheelchair really doesn't matter to me. Atticus isn't all that different from the rest of us. If you took the time to get to know him you'd realize that."

Bobby shrugged, gave me a half-hearted "I guess" and left it at that. I knew he really didn't understand, and it bothered me. I didn't push the issue. Though I didn't like when people labeled Atticus, I was enjoying the cuddling and the talking and didn't want to get into a debate about the merits of my ex-boyfriend at that exact moment in time.

Then, seemingly out of nowhere...

"Kathleen, the reason I was so excited about tonight was because I wanted to do this for the first time with someone I loved......and I love you."

My heart jumped. No, it catapulted. It did a dozen flips. Maybe more! Did he actually say what I think he just said? Maybe I didn't hear him right. Of course I didn't! I almost laughed out loud at my misplaced giddiness. Bobby pulled me closer; I nestled my head under his chin.

"You love me too, right Kathleen?"

Oh my God!

I knew he was expecting an answer, but all I could think about was "Bobby O'Hara loved me!" I selfishly basked in the warm glow of being loved by the most popular boy in the 11th grade, maybe even the entire school. My thoughts were abruptly interrupted by my name, barely a whisper from Bobby's lips.

"Kathleen?"

I couldn't look at him. It was easier to just nod my head and snuggle deeper into the crook of his neck, convincing myself that if I didn't actually say the words maybe it wasn't really a lie. It was one thing to be excited about being loved by Bobby O'Hara, yet quite another to actually love him back. I had spent years falling in love with Atticus. Did I love Bobby? To be honest, I wasn't sure, but I was enjoying the possibility all the same.

It didn't take long for the rumors to reach my ears. The rumors about *that* Saturday night. Although I assured Abby there was *nothing* to know, she eyed me suspiciously whenever Bobby and I were together, trying to note some change in our behavior toward one another, some indefinable touch, or look, that indicated we had done *it*, at least once.

Even Atticus looked at me differently. On the few occasions we talked, he barely looked up at me. I missed seeing those clear blue eyes that always told me so much.

If Abby and Atticus were wondering, everyone else just assumed. Just like they had with Sara. Except I wasn't Sara. I wasn't comfortable with the assumption and certainly didn't feel that having sex gave me any kind of special cache.

I know Bobby didn't necessarily mind the illusion of yet another conquest. In a nod to my concerns, he promised to set the record straight to anyone who asked. Short of announcing our still intact virginity at a pep rally, I guess that would have to do.

Unfortunately, all of the speculation and gossip put a strain on our relationship. The timetable for "doing it" was always hanging in the air, a conversation waiting to be had, an event waiting to be planned. Bobby's profession of love only served to fuel his desire to go all the way, because "it was time" and I was "the one." I stifled the urge to remind him that maybe his raging hormones might have something to do with it. I, on the other hand, was more than happy to stay on 2nd base, even though my own hormones had definitely made their presence known. The push and pull was more than our fledgling romance could bear and we fought constantly, everything indirectly related to this potential milestone in our sexual development.

It made me sad. I genuinely liked Bobby. I was wistful for the days when he'd walk me home from the book shop and we simply talked, enjoying the sheer pleasure of getting to know one another, accompanied by gentle butterflies in the pits of our stomachs. A sign of our mutual, and at the time, somewhat forbidden attraction.

I didn't know what to do. Part of me wondered what it would be like to be with Bobby in that way. Before *that* Saturday night, as I had begun to refer to it with Abby, I found myself utterly lost in his kisses, his touch. I realized there were times when my body was most definitely ruling my mind and I would have been perfectly willing to let things go where they might. And yet, once the status of my virginity became the focus of not only Bobby's attention but, seemingly everyone else in my high school, I became less excited by the prospect.

Torn, I turned to the one person who had always helped me make sense of the world. On a clear, crisp, sun-soaked Sunday morning, I called Atticus. My stomach felt a little like jelly from nerves, which was odd to me. To calm myself down I counted the rings until he picked up. It took three, almost four, before I heard his voice on the other end of the line.

If he was surprised to hear from me, he didn't let on.

"Hey, how are you?" he asked. His voice indicated it was not out of some polite form of conversation, but because he really cared how I was. That was Atticus,

"I don't know how I am," was my honest reply.

"Hmmmmmm, that doesn't sound good."

He didn't pry, didn't ask for details. Just waited for me to continue.

"Can we take a walk, and talk a little?" I realized how much I missed him, and started to panic that he'd turn me down.

"Sure, but I have something to do around three so can we go now?"

There was a catch in his voice that I barely picked up on. I was just so happy knowing I would see him. I offered to walk to his house but he said he'd meet me at mine since he was going in that direction later in the day.

At a half-past noon, he was at my kitchen door and we decided to grab some lunch at the local Friday's.

I was grateful for an empty house as I didn't want to explain Atticus' appearance that day. My mom often remarked how it seemed a shame that Atticus and I never saw each other anymore. Funny, because she used to worry that I saw him too much. I knew she had her issues with my dating Atticus. Once I started seeing Bobby, she seemed less judgmental about my love life, less concerned that I was too young to be getting so serious with someone. I knew why. She felt Bobby was more my "type." I knew exactly what she meant. Even so, I think she missed Atticus too.

Neither of us had had breakfast so we were both starving when we got to Friday's. We talked about so much that for a while I forgot what I really wanted to discuss. It had been a long time since we'd last been alone like this and there was obviously a lot of ground to cover. I felt guilty for letting my relationship with Bobby get in the way of my friendship with Atticus. Bobby never made me feel like I couldn't stay friends with Atticus. I was just so consumed with all things Bobby, and his circle of friends, that I let other things in my life slide. Truth be told, even Abby and I didn't spend as much time together as we used to.

After about an hour, as we were stuffing our cheeseburger deluxes into our mouths, there was a lull in our conversation. I was about to share with Atticus the reason for my call but he beat me to the punch

He grew somewhat serious, and said, "I have something to tell you."

I had been so absorbed in my own drama I never suspected Atticus might have some big news of his own.

I smiled, waiting for him to go on.

"I've met someone, someone I really like."

For a minute I didn't understand what he was saying. Atticus had a few good friends but he had trouble letting people in, especially after we'd started high school. I thought he was telling me he found a new best friend. I was curious to know who it was.

"Ok," I said, not sure how I was supposed to react, and not necessarily happy that I was about to be displaced. Even though Atticus and I had drifted apart, I guess I always felt like we were still best friends.

He just stared at me. When he said nothing and raised his eyebrows, I knew. Atticus didn't meet a new best friend, he met a new girlfriend.

"Oh," I said, feeling a little weak in the knees even though I was sitting down, the shock evident in my tone. Atticus had a new girlfriend. Why was I surprised?

Had I become like everyone else and just assumed it wasn't likely, that no one would want to date a kid in a wheelchair? The thought made me cringe. But I knew in the back of my mind, there was a part of me that felt that way, as if I would never have to worry about his finding someone else. At least not now, in high school, where no girl other than myself could have looked beyond the wheelchair to the person, at least not enough to date him. Oh my God, what an asshole I was.

Still Atticus said nothing. I was embarrassed by my reaction and tried to cover my tracks.

"Well, that's great for you. Is it someone I know?" I asked with a forced smile.

Atticus shook his head. He looked sad to me.

"No, nobody you know. She doesn't go to our school. That's who I am meeting up with at three." He said it as if that would explain everything. I sensed that even though he wanted to tell me, he didn't feel inclined to offer up any more, which of course made me want to know every detail.

I stifled the urge to ask any questions even though I had already formed a mile long list in my mind.

He changed the subject, bringing the focus back to me.

"So what did you want to talk about?" he asked, looking at his cell phone to check the time.

I shrugged. It didn't seem all that important anymore. My mind raced with images of Atticus laughing with someone else, sharing secrets with someone else, dissecting his aunt's mystery Thanksgiving dinner with someone else. Is this how he felt when he saw me kissing Bobby? It totally sucked.

"Come on Kathleen, don't do this," he implored. "What's bothering you?"

What's bothering me? My indecision over having sex with Bobby seemed to fade into the background. Now I sat there wondering if Atticus was having sex with his new girlfriend. I knew for a fact that Atticus could have sex. His legs didn't work, but we often joked that everything else down there seemed to be functioning perfectly, evidence of which I often felt against my leg, or my stomach, after we'd been kissing for a while. Thinking of kissing Atticus made me smile,

"What are you thinking?" he asked noticing the upward curve of my lips.

I couldn't tell him. What would be the point?

"We've come a long way since kindergarten," I said, hoping he wouldn't notice the crack in my voice.

He looked down at the table, then back into my eyes, his clear blue eyes like a magnet I couldn't pull away from.

"Not exactly where I thought we'd end up," he said quietly, then motioned for the bill.

I spent the entire afternoon torturing myself with images of Atticus and his new girlfriend. What did she look like? Where did she live? How did they meet? How long had they been together? Did he love her? The distraction helped me stop thinking about my Bobby dilemma, but added a new one to the mix. Maybe I still loved Atticus.

That night Bobby and I went to the movies. We shared popcorn. We held hands. We kissed. We snuggled. After the movies, we parked in our usual spot and kissed some more. There were dozens of girls who would have traded places with me in an instant. All I knew was that I didn't want to be there. It annoyed me that Bobby didn't seem to notice my mood; in his defense, I was trying to act as if nothing was wrong. Still, he was my boyfriend. Shouldn't he know me better than that? Atticus would have noticed as soon as he picked me up.

There it was. The inevitable Atticus comparison. I used to

do it much more in the beginning of my relationship with Bobby. One time I even wrote out a list comparing the two of them. A list, which very clearly indicated that Atticus was a better match for me. A list which I promptly crumpled up and threw away because I liked going out with the most popular boy in school, even if I was embarrassed to admit it to myself. A list which I carried in my heart because I knew it revealed something I didn't want to hear, something I knew one day would make more sense than it did now.

Bobby dropped me off early and I could tell he finally realized something wasn't quite right. Thankfully, he didn't question me. Instead, he gave me a kiss on the cheek, told me he'd call me when he got home, and mumbled a rushed "love you" as I got out of the car. He'd been doing that of late, and it was painfully obvious I hadn't reciprocated the words. I couldn't even manage a "me too." I smiled at his words, hoping somehow that would continue to be enough until I knew what I was really feeling.

My mom was in the living room reading one of her beloved romance novels and I plopped myself down on the couch next to her. She pretended not to be surprised by my behavior but I knew she was already wondering what was up.

I made a pathetic attempt at small talk.

"Is that book any good?"

She nodded, turned down one of the page corners, closed the book, and said, "Atticus stopped by while you were out."

"He did?" I answered, a little too quickly, a little too excited. Why hadn't he tried my cell? Or sent me a text? "What did he say?"

It took her a moment too long to answer, as if she had to think about it, but she simply replied, "Just to call him whenever you got home."

I jumped up, anxious to get to my room and do just that. I was too happy about Atticus wanting to talk to me to put much thought into my mom's hesitation.

"Kathleen?"

I stopped in my tracks and turned in the direction of my mom's voice.

"Yeah?"

She started to say something, then changed her mind.

"What?" I asked, a peculiar sense of alarm spreading through me. I wasn't sure I wanted to hear what she had to say.

"Be careful," she whispered, her voice so low I could barely hear her. I felt like there was something else. Something she wasn't telling me.

I nodded slowly, not sure if I understood exactly what she meant. She smiled at me, then opened her book and started reading once more.

"Mom?" I asked softly. "Are you okay?"

She looked up at me and smiled again. "Kathleen, if you're okay then I'm okay. Just remember how much I love you."

I waited for more because I wasn't sure she had answered my question.

"I'm fine. Go call Atticus." She waved me away with her hand and returned to her book.

I raced upstairs, pressing one on my speed dial as I went. All thoughts of anything out of the ordinary were wiped from my head when Atticus answered on the first ring. I was just so happy to hear his voice.

"Hi!" I grinned into the phone, breathless from my sprint up the stairs.

"Hi," he replied a little less enthusiastically.

"My mom said you stopped by," I continued. "What's up?"

His response was almost too fast, as if he'd been waiting to get it off his chest.

"I just wanted to make sure you were okay."

He wanted to make sure I was okay? He didn't give me a chance to comment.

"I wanted to tell you sooner, about Jennie, I just didn't know how to bring it up."

Jennie. Her name was Jennie.

He wanted to tell me sooner? How long had he been seeing her?

"It's okay," I stammered. "I'm okay."

It wasn't okay. I wasn't okay.

"I wanted to tell you right after I met her," Atticus offered with, in my opinion, a bit too much excitement in his voice. "You were always the person I wanted to tell first about everything."

Were? Is Jennie that person now?

"So how did you meet?" I asked, not really sure how the words formed on my lips. I wanted to know every detail now, as if that would somehow unravel the knot in the pit of my stomach.

Atticus prattled on about making some deliveries for his uncle, and Jennie being the daughter of one of his clients. He sounded so...happy.

"I'm glad you're okay with it. I know it was stupid to worry. It's just that I remember how I felt, even though this is different."

The reference to the Bobby situation made me feel bad. But Atticus' next words made me feel even worse.

"She's great. I can't wait for you to meet her!"

My call waiting beeped and I was thankful for the interruption. Bobby's number flashed on the screen of my cell.

"I gotta go, Bobby's calling," I said, a little more defensively than I wanted to.

"Okay. I'm glad you're cool with this. You're still one of my best friends, Kathleen. Even though we don't talk so much anymore. I hope you know that."

One of? One of? When did I become only one of his best friends? When Jennie came along?

"Yeah, I'm cool. I gotta go Atticus," and I clicked into my call with Bobby.

When we hung up that night I told Bobby I loved him.

Chapter Six

Over the next couple of weeks I obsessed about Atticus. Well, I obsessed about Jennie more. Poor Abby bore the brunt of it, though Bobby was definitely feeling my distance, which I guess was odd to him on the heels of my "I love you." He didn't question it and I didn't try to explain. Abby, on the other hand, had had enough.

"Kathleen, you have to stop this," she admonished one morning as we were sitting under the umbrella tree. "You are making yourself crazy, and you are making *me* crazy. You're with Bobby. Why is this Atticus thing bothering you so much?"

"It's not bothering me," I replied defiantly. "I'm just curious about this Jennie girl. Atticus is so sensitive; I don't want him to get hurt."

"Oh please," said Abby, rolling her eyes.

"Well, this girl probably doesn't even know him that well. Do you really think she's into him? I mean, it's hard being with Atticus."

The look on Abby's face was almost triumphant.

"Why is it hard being with Atticus?" she asked innocently, knowing full well what I meant.

I blushed in response, embarrassed.

"You didn't think anyone else would ever be with him, did you? You thought he'd always be there for you."

Her words cut like a knife. I, who had always championed Atticus' normalcy, had begun to look at him with different eyes. When did that happen? Did I really not worry about his meeting someone else because he was in a wheelchair? Did I really believe he'd always be there for me, in case I ever decided to go back? If he hadn't told me about Jennie, would I be feeling like this now?

I looked at Abby, unsure what to say. I was confused by all of it. My feelings for Bobby, my feelings for Atticus.

The morning bell rang and Abby pulled me to my feet.

"Come on, we can talk more about it later," she said, resigned. "I don't know why I put up with you!"

She laughed, shaking her head, trying to snap me out of my sullenness.

"Maybe if you're lucky, at lunch I'll tell you all about my kiss with Tyler Smith."

It felt good to listen to Abby share her "kiss" story. It felt good to be thinking of something else other than Atticus and Bobby and Jennie.

"So," Abby continued, "Tyler wants to go out this weekend and I thought maybe we could double. Do you think Bobby would be okay with that?"

I really didn't care whether or not Bobby would be okay with it. A double date with Abby sounded fun. Tyler was a nice guy, and Bobby was fairly easy going, though more so around his basketball friends. Besides, I thought hanging out with Tyler and Abby might take the pressure off Bobby and me. In spite of my distant behavior, ever since I told him I loved him he seemed to be back on the "doing it" track.

"Sounds good!" I said happily. "Let's just plan it for Saturday night. Bobby and I were going to the movies anyway, so you guys can come too."

Abby smiled.

As if reading her thoughts, I knew she was thinking we had never been on a double date before, and she was hopeful this meant we'd get to spend more time together, assuming Bobby and Tyler hit it off. They knew each other, but Bobby tended to hang with the jocks and Tyler was a stage crew junkie. I also knew for a fleeting moment Abby realized Tyler and Atticus would probably have more in common but she wouldn't dare mention it to me.

"What are you thinking?" I asked, as Abby drifted off into her thoughts.

"Oh, nothing really. Just that it's going to be so much fun!" Abby clapped her hands in excitement and I laughed at her child-like gesture. Inside I had a gnawing feeling that Bobby wouldn't be as happy.

Later that night Bobby proved me right.

"But I don't want to go on a double date. I like being with just you," he whined through the phone. I could almost see him pouting as he said it.

"It'll be fun," I said more brightly than I felt, sensing an argument in my immediate future. "Tyler's nice. And you like Abby." I tried to count in my mind the number of times I had actually ever spoken to Tyler.

"I don't even know who Tyler is," Bobby answered, making no comment about Abby.

"He's on the stage crew," I offered weakly, as if that would help him figure it out.

"Stage crew?" he snorted. "You mean he's a play geek?"

I rolled my eyes in silent exasperation. Sometimes Bobby could be such a jerk.

"Some of those play geeks are kinda funny," I said in defense of play geeks everywhere, wincing a little when I used the term. Being with Atticus had made me sensitive to labels. I thought about Kevin Jones in my history class. He was the lead in our school play last year and he always made us laugh, even if he was a little dorky. I decided not to use that example with Bobby. I knew it wouldn't matter.

"Whatever," said Bobby, obviously bored with the conversation. I refused to let it go. It suddenly became even more important to me to go out with them. We never went out with my friends, only Bobby's. It had never bothered me before. Until now.

"Well, I already told Abby we would go to the movies with them," I informed him firmly, daring him to say we couldn't.

Bobby's tone softened. "Come on Kath, do we have to?"

My tone hardened. "Yes, we have to. I want to. It's just the movies. Why are you making such a big deal?"

"Okay, okay, just the movies then," he agreed reluctantly, and quickly changed the subject. "You heard about Sara's party next weekend, right?"

Of course I had heard about the party, but I wasn't done talking about Saturday.

"Bobby, what's the big deal about the movies?"

"Oh just drop it. I said I would go. Isn't that what you wanted?"

"But why don't *you* want to go? You don't even know Tyler. Maybe you'll like him."

"Exactly my point. I don't know Tyler. Why would I want to hang out with him? I have my friends. I don't need new ones."

It was true. Bobby had been hanging out with the same group of boys for a really long time. Maybe it was a guy thing. But I thought it was more of a "play geek" thing. Bobby didn't hang out with play geeks.

I decided to quit while I was ahead. He agreed to go. Maybe he'd wind up liking Tyler. For all I knew Abby wouldn't be with him for very long and it wouldn't even matter. I circled back around to Sara's party.

"So who's going to the party?" I asked, even though I really didn't care. Bobby and I certainly wouldn't be there. Sara had made it more than clear that I was the enemy.

"The whole team. She invited us too you know."

I laughed, "Yeah, right," I said sarcastically.

"No, really, she did. She texted me today."

How long had Sara been texting Bobby? He'd never mentioned it before.

I ignored the obvious question and asked, "Do you wanna go?"

"Nah, Sara's parties are overrated," he replied to my immense relief.

I wouldn't know, I thought wryly, since I hadn't been to one since junior high. I thought back to that very first party in 6th grade. It felt like forever ago.

"I really wanted to dance with you that night," he said, startling me back into the present.

I pretended not to know what he meant. "What night?" I asked, a little surprised he remembered.

"In 6th grade. At Sara's party. I wanted to dance with you. But I was too afraid to ask you."

For a moment I forgot we had been arguing. It was still hard for me to imagine Bobby O'Hara being nervous about asking me—or anyone—to dance, though the better I got to know him, the more I realized he had this vulnerable side that totally got under my skin, in a good way. I felt like I was the only one he showed it to; it made me like him all the more.

"Abby said you wanted to but I didn't believe her," I said, still a little shocked that it was true. Mentioning Abby's name made me think about the double date, and I felt bad all over again.

"Well, you could have asked *me* to dance," he said, as if that would have been the most natural thing in the world.

I laughed and decided it was easier to just move on from the movies conversation. I didn't feel like being upset with Bobby. Especially since I was confident Atticus and this Jennie person probably never fought. It wasn't Atticus' style. He was the most agreeable person I had ever met.

"Okay, at the next party we go to I'll be sure to ask you to dance," I said trying to sound like everything was fine and letting him know I was willing to go.

"Make sure it's a slow dance," came Bobby's reply.

Saturday night rolled around and Bobby was surprisingly nice about going to the movies with Abby and Tyler. It almost made me suspicious. Since he was the only one of us with a license, we picked Tyler up at Abby's house and got to the movies at 7:00 pm.

Abby and I found seats while Bobby and Tyler got popcorn, candy, and soda. I had never paid much attention to Tyler but he didn't look like a play geek to me. I actually thought he was pretty cute. Abby chatted on excitedly about how much she liked him. It made me happy to see her so happy. I realized again how much I missed her.

I was just starting to think the night was going to go smoothly when I saw them. Abby felt me stiffen and followed my gaze.

Atticus...and a girl I assumed was Jennie. They came down the aisle to my right. She was laughing at something Atticus said...and they were holding hands. I felt like throwing up.

Abby squeezed my hand as I watched Atticus and Jennie make their way down the aisle. At that precise moment, Bobby and Tyler arrived with our snacks. Bobby was so absorbed in his conversation with Tyler that he didn't notice

Atticus. I welcomed the distraction and was glad Tyler and Bobby were actually having a decent conversation. It seemed they had found some common ground, both being big fans of the WWE. Who would have guessed.

Bobby sat next to me and I absent-mindedly reached into the popcorn tub. He was saying something but I wasn't paying attention. I was trying to see what Atticus and Jennie were doing. I always felt the section reserved for people in wheelchairs was too close to the screen, having sat there with Atticus many times before. I wondered if Jennie felt the same way.

I tried to focus on Bobby; when the Coming Attractions came on, I pretended I wanted to watch them. Bobby slipped his hand around my shoulder and I sunk into him a little, trying to make it less obvious my attention was elsewhere.

Jennie's head was turned slightly toward Atticus, as if she was listening intently to whatever he was saying. Then she laughed. And he laughed. And then...she put her head on his shoulder!

I could feel Abby's eyes on me from the next seat. She had been watching them too.

I felt a little dizzy and chugged down my soda, hoping the sugar would balance me out.

I couldn't tell you a single thing about the movie. The movie I watched that night played only in my head, and it starred Kathleen and Atticus. It started in kindergarten, led up to *that* kiss, and ended with Atticus and I getting married and having kids and being happy. It made me cry. It was fortunate Abby and I had dragged the boys to a chick flick, because every girl in the theatre was crying at some point.

Though probably not Jennie. I don't think she saw much of the movie, either. She was too busy kissing Atticus.

As the credits rolled, I stood to leave. Bobby was stretching and not getting up, which annoyed me. I wanted to leave as quickly as possible. I didn't want to see Atticus. I didn't want to see Jennie. I wanted to *go*.

Abby feigned an urgent need to pee and pushed me over Bobby's feet into the aisle.

I really did have to pee, though I debated holding it in until we got somewhere else. What if Jennie had to go too? I wondered then if she even knew who I was. We didn't go to the same school. And while I am sure Atticus would have mentioned me, I doubt he would have shown her a picture. Maybe bumping into her in the bathroom wouldn't be such a bad thing. I'd sort of have the advantage.

"Come on," I said to Abby, grabbing her hand and pulling her toward the crowded restroom.

"I don't really have to go," she protested, not understanding my sudden desire to *stay*.

"I do," I said. We planted ourselves at the end of a very long line, and I watched.

"Kathleen, what are you up to?" Abby asked, her eyes starting to search as well. She didn't need to ask. She knew.

The line moved slowly, and sure enough, along came Jennie, Atticus by her side. She was only a few people behind me and I heard her tell Atticus she would meet him at the front door of the theatre. He started to turn away, but something made him stop and look down the line. Our eyes locked. His widened just a bit. I thought he was going to say hello, but instead he turned back to Jennie and said, "Wow, long line."

She laughed, commenting on how it was always the case with the girls' room, and he headed toward the entrance to the theatre.

Jennie didn't notice a thing. I felt his perceived snub quite keenly and immediately texted Atticus my feelings about it.

"wtf – not even a hello?"

"u caught me by surpriz – I panicked"

"rude"

Abby grabbed my phone when she realized what I was doing.

"Stop this, Kathleen, just stop it. You are acting like a baby."

My plan to secretly spy on Jennie hadn't started off so well.

Bobby and Tyler walked up to us.

"You guys are still on line?" Bobby asked incredulously.

"No, we're just standing here for fun," I snapped. He held up his hands in mock defense.

"Whoa, don't mess with a girl when she has to pee," he said, trying to make a joke.

I smiled weakly and Tyler suggested we meet them at,

where else, the front door of the theatre, which we would get to before Jennie, and where Atticus would be waiting. I didn't want to face him again.

"You know what, let's just go, this line is ridiculous," I decided. "I think the mall is still open and I need to pick up some hair clips," I added quickly. The entrance to the mall was on the back side of the theatre.

"Now?" Bobby asked.

I nodded, explaining how they were on sale and today was the last day and I had forgotten all about it until now.

Tyler and Bobby shrugged and renewed their wrestling conversation while they walked in the direction of the mall.

I sighed, relieved. Abby and I hurried past them so we could hopefully catch the Claire's accessory store before it closed.

In spite of the Atticus sighting, it was a fun night. We went to Friday's in the mall after our unplanned pit stop to buy the clips. I got some really cute ones and they were actually on sale! When Bobby dropped me off at 11:30, he said he was surprised about what a good time he had.

"See, I told you so," I chided, "We geeks aren't so bad."

He looked at me, his brow furrowed. "You're not a geek!"

I laughed, and he continued, "I draw the line at dating geeks."

I raised an eyebrow, not quite sure if he was serious, and he leaned in to kiss me goodnight.

It was a nice kiss. For a moment, I forgot about Atticus and Jennie and simply enjoyed the pleasure of kissing Bobby. It was nearing my curfew when I pulled away, knowing how easily we could get caught up in more kissing, and how more kissing quickly led to other things. Lately, when I felt those feelings, it confused me more than ever.

"I have to get going," I said, as convincingly as I could.

Bobby groaned and made me promise we wouldn't make a habit of the double date.

"I like having you all to myself."

My stomach flipped in a good way, and a bad one. I didn't know why. I jumped out of the car and waved. "Call me in the morning."

"I love you," Bobby's replied.

"I love you, too," I answered, more out of habit than real

emotion. It was easier to just say it than to sort out my feelings and figure out if I really meant it, as least for now.

My cell rang at midnight, just as I was falling asleep, trying hard not to let Atticus and Jennie haunt my dreams. Sometimes when Bobby and I ended the night with just a kiss, he would call and tell me stuff. Stuff that would make me blush. I answered on the second ring, trying not to wake up completely.

"Hey, I was just about to fall asleep. "

"Well that was weird, huh?"

I shook the sleep out of my head and looked at the caller ID to make sure I had heard right. It was Atticus.

I woke up fast, but it still took me a few seconds to gather my thoughts.

"What was that about? Why didn't you say hello." I was hurt.

"I don't know, Katie. I froze. I wasn't ready for you guys to meet."

"Why not?"

"I haven't really told her about you."

I wasn't sure what to make of that. I asked the same question again.

"Why not?"

Atticus was silent for a while. I imagined him deep in thought, his blue eyes searching for the right way to answer my question. Atticus rarely spoke before he knew exactly what he wanted to say. Usually I was patient about his thought process, but not tonight,

"Why not, Atticus?" I added his name to emphasize my annoyance.

Atticus exhaled into the phone, and, in measured speech, continued.

"Katie, if I talk about you, she'll know." His voice trailed off.

I felt a single butterfly flutter in my stomach. Know what? Know what? I screamed the question silently but I didn't say a word to Atticus. I just waited.

I could feel his struggle. It sent my heart racing, making me certain of the words that would come next, but unsure I wanted to hear them.

"She'll know that I still love you, Katie."

Neither of us said a word for a long while after that. But it wasn't an uncomfortable silence. It was as if we were both enjoying the moment, the secret pleasure of all we shared, and the unspoken promise of what could have been, what could still be. It reminded me of nights when we'd fall asleep on the phone, neither of us wanting to say goodbye, soothed by the breathing we heard on the other end of the line, wrapping us in the warmth of a hug just as sure as if we'd been lying next to one another on my bed.

My call waiting beeped in and I saw that it was Bobby. I didn't want to answer.

It felt good to hear those words from Atticus, especially after witnessing his movie-long make-out session with Jennie.

My happiness was short-lived.

"Listen, Kathleen." The switch back to Kathleen raised a red flag. I wasn't going to like what was coming.

"I will always love you. You were my first real friend, my first girlfriend, my best friend for as long as I have known you. But I really like Jennie. A lot. For a long time I used to think you were the only person that really *got* me. Jennie gets me too. It feels good. I don't want to mess things up with her."

I wondered how I could feel so high and so low within a matter of minutes. I didn't know what to say. It was all so confusing. Bobby. Atticus. Jennie. All of it.

The tears were upon me before I had a chance to try and keep them in check. Big, round sobs. Not soft, dainty, sniffles but an ugly, loud crying jag. I couldn't stop.

Atticus switched back to Katie mode immediately.

"Katie, Katie, what? What? Why are you crying?"

My call waiting beeped again. I didn't even check to see who it was. I knew it was Bobby. I didn't want to talk to anyone. Not even Atticus.

"I have to go," I told him quickly and hung up the phone before he changed my mind.

He called me back three times, but I didn't answer.

I lay for a long time just thinking about all of it, trying to sort through the maze of my feelings. I tried to be logical. Of course I still cared for Atticus. He was my first love. You never really forget your first love. And I really liked Bobby, too. He made me feel such different emotions than Atticus. Did that make those feelings more or less real I wondered.

I looked at the clock. It was almost one in the morning. I knew what I had to do. As I got up from the bed, I felt like I was watching myself in a movie. Surely I wasn't *really* going to do this?

I walked out of my room and down the hall.

When I knocked on the door, I got the sense she was expecting me.

"Mom, can we talk?"

I sat on the bed and collapsed into her arms, grateful my dad had fallen asleep on the couch that night watching TV.

"I'm still in love with Atticus."

A hug had never felt so good.

The next morning the "feel good breakfast" aroma was in full effect. Mom was in the kitchen humming away and dad and the boys were already working on their second helping of pancakes.

I knew mom loved these family moments. She was secretly pleased when both of my brothers decided to stay local for college, a Division 3 school which enabled them to play football instead of keeping the bench warm somewhere else.

I sat down at the table just as a new batch of pancakes was placed on the serving plate, and I realized I was incredibly hungry. I yawned a good morning and dug in, careful to avoid my mother's gaze, not quite ready to acknowledge the uncharacteristic talk we'd had the night before.

The men were oblivious as usual, lost in their meal, though my dad tousled my hair a bit, the way he did when I was a little girl. I let him.

His attempt at small talk was heartfelt.

"Did you have a good time at the movies?" he asked.

I nodded.

My brothers excused themselves so they could get to the gym. Even when they didn't have practice or a game, they continued their workout regimens religiously, both still harboring unfulfilled dreams of playing for The Fighting Irish.

I imagine at some point shortly after that my mom gave my dad "the look", the one that meant his presence was no longer needed, because he got up mumbling something about raking up the leaves.

It wasn't a Saturday morning, but I sensed a Saturday morning talk was in my immediate future.

"So?" she asked, cocking her head to one side. "Things looking a little brighter today?"

I nodded, surprised that it was true. It's amazing what sleep can do for the soul. I was still upset, but felt like I had a little more direction, or clarity. When my mom hugged me the night before, it all just came tumbling out, like an avalanche. Once I started I couldn't stop. My mom just listened, nodded, and told me she loved me. She didn't offer any advice other than to sleep on it. Which I did. Now it was her turn to talk and my turn to listen. Over pancakes.

For two hours, she told me about her boyfriend, the one that had died in the car accident, the one she had planned her life with, who's name *she* had practiced her name with, over and over again. She told me how she thought she'd never stop feeling the pain, the loss, the love. But she did when she met my dad and life presented a new chapter for her. She hadn't wanted to open that book, but her mother told her it was time. Time to move forward even if she never quite forgot the past.

"Atticus called earlier while you were asleep."

I glanced at my cell, confused. It hadn't rung all morning.

"He wanted to talk to me, not you," my mom replied to my unspoken question. She continued, slowly, as if choosing her words carefully. "He was pretty upset, Kathleen; and he was worried about you."

He was upset? Why was Atticus upset? He was the one who was with his new girlfriend and ignored *me*.

I sensed a shift in the direction of the conversation, as if my mom was trying to read me to determine exactly what she was going to say. I didn't like the feeling it gave me and I averted my gaze to my empty plate.

"Kathleen?" She said my name as a question, as if I'd disappeared from her sight. "He didn't mean to hurt you. He remembered how it felt when you started dating Bobby."

I just stared at the back of my hands, picking the chipped nail polish off of my two-week old manicure with unusual gusto.

"He did say you would always be special to him." The way she said it made it sound like a consolation prize.

I finally looked up because I couldn't help feeling there was something my mom wasn't telling me. I wanted to see her eyes to confirm my suspicions. "Did he say anything else?"

She started to speak and then shook her head slowly from side to side.

There was only one thing I wanted to know. "He doesn't love me anymore, does he? He wants to be with Jennie, doesn't he?" The questions made my heart ache.

She looked away for a second then faced me once again. Was she trying to protect me from the answers or was there something more?

"You've got to let him go, Kathleen. He's moved on. And so have you. A first love is always special. You will always remember it. But you will have many loves in your future. Go find them."

It was good advice. I had no choice but to accept it. Atticus no longer loved me in that way. He loved Jennie. He wanted to move on and made sure I got that message by enlisting the aid of my mom. How embarrassing! I decided then and there to cut Atticus out of my life. I know it was childish, but it was easier to just not deal with it.

Christmas was only weeks away and provided the perfect distraction. I threw myself completely into the season, becoming the ever-cheerful elf. The world around me seemed lighter and happier, and I channeled those feelings inside me as much as possible. I hadn't spoken to Atticus since the night of the movies. He'd made his choice. At least I thought he had. And I had made mine. Bobby was my boyfriend. The cutest, most popular boy in school. And he loved *me*. Isn't this what every high school girl in the world dreamed about? To be loved by the cutest, most popular boy in school?

I was reminding myself of this very fact as I was eating lunch with Abby, whom unknowingly forced me to silently repeat my new mantra over and over.

"What are you wearing to the Christmas dance?" Abby asked, not waiting for me to answer. "I don't have a thing to wear so I'm going shopping this weekend. Do you want to come?" she asked cheerfully.

I nodded yes in response but couldn't help thinking about the last time we had gone shopping for a dance. The last time I had been to a dance, I had been so excited about my secret, so happy sitting on Atticus' lap for the slow dances. It all seemed like a dream now.

Abby continued chatting almost non-stop. She was nervous about something, that much I could tell. Normal Abby was fairly reserved and quiet. Nervous Abby talked about anything and everything to avoid mentioning whatever it was that made her nervous.

After about ten minutes of her chatter I started to laugh. Abby looked at me blankly.

"What? What's so funny?" she asked, her cheeks flushed, her eyes wide. She knew she'd been found out. Abby rarely kept anything from me and I wondered what had gotten her so worked up.

"You are what's funny," I answered still laughing. "Slow down or you are going to hyperventilate."

Abby laughed uncomfortably, and I knew I didn't want to know what was making her nervous. I immediately tried to change the subject.

"I am not even close to finishing my history report, are you?"

Abby stared at me like I had two heads. It wasn't the question she was expecting.

"Ummm, yeah, I finished it up last night...when I got back from The Commons." Her voice quivered slightly at the end of her sentence.

The Commons was a strip of local shops and cafes we frequented more when the weather was warm. It struck me as odd that Abby threw that last part in, about going there. So I ignored her mention of it.

"Oh, shit, I wish I hadn't waited this long!" I complained. Abby just rolled her eyes and shook her head. I *always* waited until the last minute. We both knew it.

"They opened a new jewelry store there," Abby continued casually. "That's where I was. My mom was picking out her Christmas gift."

I wasn't big on jewelry. I shrugged, not really interested in the new jewelry store.

Abby was *very* interested in it.

"They have a lot of cute charms, I was thinking of getting some new ones for my bracelet."

"Oh, that's good. Those charm bracelets are kinda cool." I did actually like them.

Abby looked like she was going to burst. I knew I didn't

want to hear what she was going to tell me. But I was going to hear it. I put Abby out of her misery and asked the question she needed to hear from me.

"Okay Abby, what's bugging you?"

Abby looked relieved but played coy.

"Nothing, nothing..." she answered, a little too quickly, but clearly ready to burst.

"Abby, just *tell* me already!"

And burst she did, talking as quickly as I'd ever heard her.

"Well, I was in the store with my mom, and it's really pretty big and I was looking at the charms for my bracelet, and I heard his voice and I looked over and I saw...I saw...well, I saw Atticus buying one of the bracelets. He didn't see me though, or if he did he didn't say hello. But I don't think he saw me because it wouldn't be like Atticus to not say hello, and, anyway, he had the bracelet gift-wrapped and the man behind the counter asked him who it was for, which I thought was a little rude, and he said it was for someone special. The man smiled and said he made a good choice and Atticus smiled and said he hoped so, and then he left."

Abby took a much-needed breath. I, on the other hand, had a little trouble catching mine.

"I knew I shouldn't have told you," she said as she looked at my expression.

"You were dying to tell me," I said, smugly, but the look on Abby's face told me it stung her a little. I know Abby didn't tell me to hurt me. She told me because she thought I would want to know. She was right.

"It's okay, Abby. I'm glad you told me...sort of." I smiled apologetically, and she instantly perked up.

She waited for me to say something else. What was I supposed to say? I swallowed hard to get rid of the lump forming in my throat. I needed to change the subject but only partially succeeded.

"I wonder what Bobby is getting me for Christmas?" I asked with a level of excitement I really didn't feel.

Abby looked momentarily confused at my lack of comment but easily switched gears to discuss the new topic.

Bobby had always given Sara the nicest gifts—even in grade school.

Abby was about to give me her opinion when I saw her

eyes dart anxiously to the cafeteria entrance. I followed them and sure enough, there was Atticus rolling in late for lunch. His eyes caught mine and he smiled. I felt like someone had put their hand around my heart and squeezed tight.

I turned back to Abby, but her eyes continued to follow Atticus' slow progress toward our table.

"Is he coming here?" I whispered to Abby as quietly as I could.

She nodded ever so slightly, and decided it was time to get another dessert.

"No!" I reached for her arm, begging her not to leave me alone, but Abby pulled away, said a nervous hello to Atticus and left me to fend for myself.

"Am I that scary?" he asked with a smile. "You can't avoid me forever."

"Why not?" I replied, sounding less annoyed than I wanted to.

I wouldn't look at him. I couldn't look at him.

"Katie, this is silly. We can't not be friends."

"We're friends," I countered coolly. "Just not best friends anymore. It happens, right?"

I felt his eyes boring into me, but I refused to look up. I could never resist Atticus' eyes. I didn't want to see what was in them today.

"Why won't you look at me?" he asked, the hurt pouring out in his voice.

"I turned to him finally, and flatly asked, "What do you want, Atticus?" It was cold and impersonal and disclosed none of what I was actually feeling inside.

"Your mom told you I called?" he asked, a tremble in his voice.

I nodded slowly, sadly. What could I say?

"She explained it to you. About me and Jennie?"

I nodded again, at a loss for words. What did he expect me to say? It's okay he chose Jennie over me?

"Oh," he whispered, a subtle drop in his shoulders.

He shifted in his wheelchair and it was then I saw he was carrying a gift in his lap. My mind raced to the bracelet, but the box looked too large. No, the bracelet was clearly for someone else.

"I wanted you to have this." He put the box on the table.

"I hope you like it."

I nodded, mumbled my thanks, and said I had to go. I picked up the box and started to walk away. It felt wrong. It all just felt so wrong. I turned back to look at him, my expression softened a little, and thanked him again, this time apologizing for not having a gift in return. Me, who had always gotten Atticus' gift first, before anyone else's.

Abby walked over to me, eating a popsicle, curious to know about our exchange.

"What's that?" she asked, looking at the gift. I rolled my eyes at her, given the obvious answer.

"Are you gonna open it?" she asked, undaunted.

"No, not here," I replied.

"I wonder what it is?" she asked, trying to make me as interested as she was.

"Well," I replied a little too sadly, "I am pretty sure it's not a bracelet."

Abby didn't say another word.

When I got home that afternoon, I put the gift on my dresser and just stared at it. Christmas was still a week away and Atticus and I always exchanged on Christmas day. I realized he would be doing that with someone else this year.

My curiosity got the better of me and I tore off the paper.

It was a digital picture frame. I soon realized that wasn't the gift.

There was a post-it attached that read "Plug me in."

So I did.

And there we were. In every photo. Ten years of photos. Ten years of Atticus and me.

It was the best gift he had ever given me. Way better than any bracelet could ever be.

As I sat on my bed and watched the slide show, I struggled with my feelings. Why had Atticus given this to me? Did he think I would ever forget any of it? There we were at St. Mary's. At the pool. At the dance last year, me on his lap, both of us smiling so brightly, filled with the promise of puppy love.

I thought about the term: puppy love. Is that what we shared? Is that all it was? Maybe that's all he had with Jennie. Maybe that's all I had with Bobby.

The photos paraded in front of me and I felt certain what Atticus and I had shared was more than puppy love. Is that what he wanted me to see? Is that what he saw when he looked at them?

My cell rang and I absently grabbed it without looking at who the caller was.

"So, did you open it?" Abby's voice came excitedly through the phone.

I glanced back at the images fading in and out from the frame's wooden border.

"No," I lied, crossing my fingers, feeling a little guilty about not telling Abby the truth. I wanted my moment with his gift. I didn't want to talk about it, or figure it out, with anyone else. I needed time to process it myself.

"I wonder what it is," Abby's voice rose at the end of the sentence, her excitement contagious even though I already knew what the box contained.

"I'll tell you when I open it," I promised, then hung up with the excuse that my mom needed help getting dinner ready.

I stared at my phone then smiled as I hit the speed dial number that belonged to Atticus. I never took him off even though I rarely called him anymore.

He answered right away and laughed into the phone.

"You opened it!"

"It was a great gift, Atticus. Thank you."

It felt good to talk to him like this, like we had a thousand times before.

"Oh good, I'm glad." He almost sounded relieved.

"I can't believe how many photos you had. Guess we really have been friends a long time."

The warm glow of all those memories flushed my cheeks. Could he feel what I was feeling?

"I was going through some pictures I took with Jennie and I found all these old ones of us on my computer. I felt kinda guilty keeping them there, and then I saw the frame in a store and thought you might like to have them."

What did he just say? He didn't want to keep them? Why would I want them if *he* didn't? But the truth was, I *did* want them.

"You didn't keep them?" I didn't want to ask the question because I didn't want to hear his answer, but it flew out of me before I could stop it.

He didn't answer right away.

"No, no, I kept them. I downloaded them to a flash drive."
A flash drive? Was that supposed to make it okay? I'd been relegated to a flash drive?

"All of them?" Out popped another question that I didn't want to hear the answer to.

Silence. I guess he realized my mood had changed.

I answered for him. The anger in my voice chilled even me.

"Whatever, Atticus, it's okay. I just wanted to thank you for the frame and the pictures. It was really nice of you."

And then I got mean.

"If I want to delete them and add different ones, how do I do that?"

"I have the instructions. I'll give them to you." His voice sounded empty. How could it be okay for him, and not for me? I mean really, what was he thinking?

I didn't need to say anything else. He knew what I meant. I knew what I meant. I was going to delete the pictures he gave me and add pictures of Bobby and me.

After we hung up I watched the images over and over, reliving every moment, every smile. Atticus had been a part of my life for as long as I could remember and the emptiness I felt, realizing I had to let him go, was almost more than I could bear. Of course I wouldn't delete the photos. They were all I had left of him, of us.

I put the frame on my dresser and forced myself to smile. I remembered reading somewhere if you smiled on the outside it actually made you feel good on the inside. That it couldn't be helped. I tested out the theory and found there was some truth to it. I smiled at Atticus. My Atticus.

Somehow looking at the pictures gave me closure. It was time to take control of my ping ponging emotions. Maybe I was finally ready to move forward. Atticus was my past. Bobby was my future.

I sent Atticus a quick text of apology. It wasn't fair to have jumped all over him like that.

"i overreacted, pictures were great, will always cherish them and the time we spent together. Let's work on the friend thing."

At least it was a start.

I dialed Bobby's number and never looked back.

Epilogue

Here I am, back where Atticus first told me he loved me: the boys' bathroom of our high school. Graduation is only a few hours old, Atticus is headed to the airport, bound for an internship in New York and eventually Columbia University, Jennie conveniently to NYU, and I'm here wondering how I ever let him go.

During our senior year, Atticus and I remained friendly, a tenuous bond, but not like it'd been before; and a few minutes earlier he had been here with me, in our "place." Somehow it felt right. He took my hands in his and thanked me. He told me how grateful he was for that day in kindergarten, in the boys' bathroom at St. Mary by the Shore, for making him believe he was no different than anyone else. He had been really scared to come to school. Kids had been mean to him before and he didn't know what to expect. My pure acceptance of him set in motion a chain of events so subtle, and yet so powerful, that in some ways, it eventually led to Atticus leaving me. From that day forward he had never doubted himself, his ability to be like everyone else. Until I did. When he thought I chose Bobby. And I knocked the wind out of him for the very first time.

In the end, I came to realize while Atticus was in a wheelchair, I was the one who couldn't stand on my own two feet. I knew better. But I didn't fight for Atticus, didn't fight for us, no matter what my mom did or didn't tell me that day. I wanted the decision to be made for me. And it scares me to think why.

One day, maybe, I'll find my legs and run, run as fast I can toward New York and Atticus. But not now.

I clutched the digital camera in my hand. One last picture. Atticus and me in our caps and gowns, diplomas in hand.

I hurried home and added it to my frame. Bobby's graduation party started in a few hours and I had to get dressed. After all, the prom King and Queen couldn't be late.

About the Author

    As a young girl, Stephanie would write about anything and everything simply because it made her happy. She parlayed her love of the written word into a successful marketing and communications career, while a host of never submitted or unfinished picture book and romance novels clogged up her computer's hard drive. Stephanie resides in her hometown of the Bronx, NY, with her son, husband and crazy boxer pup named Bella. She continues to write simply because it makes her happy. *Kissing Atticus Primble*—which made a daring escape from her computer's hard drive—is her first published novel.